T0157146

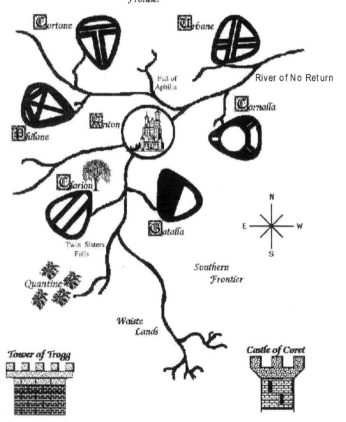

Northern
Frontier

Cortane

Urbane

Fall of
Aphilia

River of No Return

Cornalla

Triton

Dilane

Clorion

N

E   W

S

Batalla

Twin Sisters
Falls

Southern
Frontier

Quantine

Waiste
Lands

Tower of Trogg

Castle of Coret

Leprechaun Legacy
Book Two: Return to Anton

Chuck Bowers

iUniverse

LEPRECHAUN LEGACY
BOOK TWO: RETURN TO ANTON

iUniverse books may be ordered through booksellers or by contacting:

iUniverse
1663 Liberty Drive
Bloomington, IN 47403
www.iuniverse.com
1-800-Authors (1-800-288-4677)

Because of the dynamic nature of the Internet, any web addresses or links contained in this book may have changed since publication and may no longer be valid. The views expressed in this work are solely those of the author and do not necessarily reflect the views of the publisher, and the publisher hereby disclaims any responsibility for them.

Any people depicted in stock imagery provided by Thinkstock are models, and such images are being used for illustrative purposes only. Certain stock imagery © Thinkstock.

ISBN: 978-1-4917-9145-5 (sc)
ISBN: 978-1-4917-9144-8 (e)

Library of Congress Control Number: 2016903326

Print information available on the last page.

iUniverse rev. date: 2/29/2016

Acknowledgments

This work is dedicated to my friends and family. In October 2009, I was in an industrial accident. It left me in a coma for twenty-one days and in a number of hospitals for several months. Then I lived with assisted living for five years.

Thanks to my God and friends and family, I fully recovered. Then I lived in northern Michigan for a year with my best friend, Herb, and his dog, Jake. I had two strokes, which took my speech and use of my right side. With Herb and Jake's help, I was restored to near-perfect health. That brought me to the point of completing this second book in a three-part series.

I would like to thank my followers for their dedication and patience. I truly believe *Return to Anton* will prove itself worth the wait. Share the news I'm back on track and the adventure continues.

We pick up our adventures of *Leprechaun Legacy* with Alex paying a visit to the Kingdom of Anton. There are new characters and old friends. The reader is in for a colorful and action-filled thrill as Alex is introduced to leprechaun traditions and customs. The war is still heated. Find a relaxing spot to sit back and make the return journey to Anton a fun and exciting one. To get the full impact of this book, it's best the reader has read book one, *Leprechaun Legacy*, to be familiar with the characters and the underground Kingdom of Anton, but this book is a story of its own. Enjoy.

CONTENTS

CHAPTER 1
UNANSWERED QUESTION

After the terrible storm that destroyed the McNaire farmhouse, barn, and outbuildings, it was a great joy to find Alex survived the awesome ordeal. Alex only remained conscious for a short while and then fell into a deep coma. Grandfather McNaire and Thomas both took one of Alex's legs as Michael picked Alex up by the shoulders. They carried Alex to the buckboard and made him as comfortable as possible. Michael and Grandfather McNaire settled into the seat of the buckboard as Thomas remained in the back with Alex.

Michael headed the buckboard toward town and Dr. Downs's home. The doctor's house also served as his office. Here, he received his patients from the village and surrounding countryside.

The weather had changed to more seasonable temperatures. Rain clouds were forming to the east of the village—not a storm but more like the normal rain showers that were still needed. Even after the storm, the ground needed water to sink deep into the soil for the crops to grow and spread roots.

Thomas could hear Alex mumble, not a single word of which he could make sense. Once they arrived at Dr. Downs's home, they unloaded Alex and carried him into the house.

"Thomas," directed Michael, "take the rig, and fetch your mother and sisters."

"Yes, Father," replied Thomas.

The doctor called for his nurse. Then he asked Michael and Grandfather McNaire to wait in the sitting room. The doctor checked Alex from head to toe and found only a small bruise on Alex's left temple. By the time the doctor had finished his examination, the entire McNaire family was waiting anxiously in the sitting room.

As the doctor entered the room, Jean ran up to him. "Doctor, my son, Alex … is he—"

"Wait," interrupted the doctor. "Just slow down, Mrs. McNaire, please. My preliminary exam revealed very little."

"Good," said Jean.

"On the contrary," stated the doctor, "it just means I don't externally see any broken bones or cuts. However, there is a bruise on the lad's left temple, which could explain his unconscious state. With your permission, it is my opinion we should move Alex to the Yorkshire Hospital and have x-rays and a few other tests done."

Jean looked very concerned. "May I see him?" she asked.

"Sure. He seems fast asleep, so there is no way to say for sure he would hear a word you said. At the same time, he may hear every word but just not be able to respond. Closed head injuries like his have no set pattern. Please make it short, for the lad needs rest. He is probably battling to regain consciousness, which will take all his energy," the doctor said.

"All right then, Doctor," said Jean as she entered the examination room.

"Michael," said the doctor, "I'll make all the arrangements for a covered wagon. It is nearly a full day's journey to Yorkshire. You will probably need some time to make plans for your family. It could be a day, a week, or even months before Alex comes around. Though it is hard for me to tell you, he may never come around. If he does wake up, his condition will depend on how long it takes; he may not be the same lad he once was."

"Now wait, Doctor," stated Michael, "is there not a fair chance he could be the same son I've known since he was born?"

"Hear, hear," said Grandfather McNaire. "You've just said you know nothing for sure."

"Very well, you McNaires are a stubborn lot. Of course, there is that possibility. I must ready my initial reports to accompany Alex to the hospital. I will see you before his departure," said the doctor.

When the doctor had left, they all went in to see Alex. Jean wet Alex's brow with a cool cloth as Susan and Sharrie Lee went to her side. They both had tears in their eyes but were not yet crying. Thomas stood at the foot of the bed with his head hung low, as if praying. Grandfather and Michael stood at the other side of the bed, each with one arm around his own waist supporting his other arm from the elbow, holding his chin as though deep in thought.

After a while, a nurse came in and asked the family to please leave the room so she could clean Alex up and change him into a hospital gown. The McNaire family complied and left the room as the nurse began her duties.

Once in the main sitting room, Michael asked Jean how she'd like to see things go from there. "Mike, my love, how about Grandfather and me go with Alex in the covered wagon? You, Thomas, and the girls could follow in the buckboard," said Jean.

"Sounds fine, Jean, but I'm afraid that wouldn't do. Perhaps I can stop by the O'Sheys' and ask Kenneth O'Shey if he could do without Brad for a day or two. I and Thomas must round up the stock. Before that, we must mend the corral and barn doors. Brad has two brothers to help at the O'Shey stead. I'm sure Ken would help us out. Brad could drive the girls. In the meantime, Thomas could take you, Grandfather, Susan, and Sharrie to the farm and pack the things you will need for a week-or-so stay in Yorkshire. After Brad has dropped you off, give him a list of what else you need. Grandfather can ride back with Brad. Then, Thomas, he, and I will join you as soon as we can. No more than two days," concluded Michael.

"Very good," stated Jean.

The family broke up, and Grandfather and Michael stepped onto the doctor's front porch for a pipe. "Well, Michael, the lad's alive," began Grandfather. "He'll pull through this, son, as sure as the sun rises."

"Yes, Father, I believe he will do just that. Papa, where do you think the gold came from?" questioned Michael.

"Don't really know, son," replied Grandfather McNaire. "Only Alex can answer that. There is a good chance he doesn't know either. If he does, he may not be able to recall it. Remember that storm beat us down for two days and a third went by before we found the boy."

"Sure is a lot of gold," stated Michael.

"Ay," replied Grandfather.

"I'm thinking of all the good it could do."

"Yes," said Grandfather.

"I believe it should be left up to Alex to say what it is used for," suggested Michael.

"True," began Grandfather. "Until then, I'd advise it be kept quiet."

"I agree, Papa. I'll inform the others," ended Michael.

Thomas, Susan, and Sharrie Lee got onto the buckboard. Michael told them to take their time and to stop by the O'Shey farm and inquire about Brad. He also instructed them to keep the gold a secret for the time being. Tell Ken O'Shey I'll see him later today for his answer." These were Michael's parting words.

CHAPTER 2
AN UNTOLD SECRET

As Alex lay in his sickbed, his mind was in the Kingdom of Anton. In a dream state, his mind placed him in the Battle of Clarion. He could almost taste the burning hair of the giant spider that held him in a death grip. Alex relived these traumatic events. He tried to scream out for help. He did not know he was not making even a single squeak. Not even a moan or sigh passed through his lips. It seemed as if he was watching the fighting and himself from a distance. He had no control over the action taking place in his head. Not the slightest movement came from Alex. He just lay there as a lump of clay. The only indication he was alive was the rising and falling of his chest as he breathed.

Jean stayed by Alex's side. She would talk to him

awhile, weep some, and then start over again. She begged Alex to wiggle a toe or move a finger in response to her presence. Nothing happened. Jean held her son's hand and would not give up hope.

Grandfather and Michael split up on the front porch. Michael began walking down the short path to the main street of town. He looked at the damage the recent storm had caused. Almost every storefront window had been broken. A few people were boarding up their properties as a few others walked about. Michael did not pay much attention, as he was deep in thought over Alex and his own property. Of course, his son was his biggest concern. He was so deep in thought he nearly walked into Squire O'Conner's horse, on which sat the constable. Squire pulled back on the reigns of his steed to startle Michael.

"See here, Michael. What are you doing in town?" The squire dismounted and tied his horse to a hitching rail.

"It is my boy, Alex. He's been hurt and is laid up at Dr. Downs's," Michael stated.

"Ya don't say," replied the constable.

"Yes, he was caught out in the open when the storm hit. We found him in the fields this morning. The tree next to where we found him was hit by lightning. It split the massive trunk down the middle to the ground. It's a wonder Alex is with us at all," choked Michael.

"How is the lad?" asked the squire.

"Breathing and nothing more. The doctor said he has a closed head injury and is in a coma. He is sending Alex to Yorkshire Hospital. Jean is going to accompany him and my girls with Father. Thomas and I will follow tomorrow or the day after. I must first secure the farm and stock," finished Michael.

"Hold up a minute, Mike," began the squire. "Some of the single men and older boys are meeting in the morning around eight bells at what is left of the White Horse Inn. They are arranging search crews and work details. We figure together, as a village, we can gather spread-out stock and do enough repairs to the homes that were damaged to make them livable. Things should get close to normal quicker. It's getting late in the season for crops. We can get it in shape as a group quicker than as individual families running around the countryside. Ya have your mark on your stock, Michael?" asked the constable.

"Yes, of course," answered Michael.

"Well then, join your missus and family. Leave the farm to us, and don't spend your time worrying about things here. As in the time of our ancestors, your neighbors are near to see us through times like these," finished Squire O'Conner.

"Thank you, Shane," said Michael. Shane was the squire's first name, though seldom used. "I'll take you up on that offer and leave Thomas to help. Nothing for the lad to do except sit around in Yorkshire. Helping around here will keep him occupied—perhaps keep him from worrying too much about his brother," concluded Michael.

Grandfather McNaire strolled along the small stream that ran through the backyard of Dr. Downs's property. It was filled with fresh rainwater, which ran quickly over the larger stones in its bed. Grandfather, though deeply concerned about Alex, could not help but wonder about the gold—not so much the tremendous amount but where it came from and how Alex fit into the picture. Grandfather knew that deplumes were very, very old. They had no dates and varied in weight. They were made from melting gold nuggets, pouring the molten liquid into molds, and then dipping them in water to cool until the liquid hardened. This was an ancient form of minting coins. Each coin's worth would be determined by its weight in grams. Then the age factor would determine its overall value. A single deplume was enough to make a family of seven very rich. Alex had one on him, and Thomas had discovered nineteen more wrapped in Alex's handkerchief in the downed tree's trunk.

Oh, yes, thought Grandfather, *Alex knew where and how the fortune came to be. The secrets lie with Alex.*

Grandfather had heard many tales about pots of gold—tales so old their endings had long been forgotten. As he reflected on such stories, he began to ponder the possibilities. At that very moment, he made up his mind something truly out of the ordinary had happened to Alex, much more than what seemed apparent.

Michael and Grandfather joined each other on the front porch. "Good timing," said Grandfather McNaire.

"Yes, Father, and I have some good news," said Michael. After Michael filled his father in on the new plans, the two sat on the front porch swing, packed their pipe bowls, and smoked.

"Michael," questioned Grandfather, "where are ya hiding the gold?"

"Ya know, I haven't even thought about it. It would be a good idea; besides, the weight of it is bruising me legs. I've split it between me two front pockets. Papa, should we take one along with us to Yorkshire? I'm sure we'd get a better value there than here in our small county," finished Michael.

"No," shouted Grandfather, "absolutely not! Son, it wouldn't be wise. To take gold that old to Yorkshire would be a grave mistake. People here would know about it before you could return home. To travel with such valuables on an open road is just inviting thieves to rob you. Besides, don't you think we should wait on Alex? After all, it does look as if he found the lot."

"True on all accounts, Father," replied Michael, puffing on his pipe.

Grandfather's eyebrows wrinkled, a sign the old man was thinking hard. "Yes, Michael, I think I know a good place for the deplumes," stated Grandfather McNaire. "I was going to let you know of the location someday soon anyway: the old cedar chest in my room, the one that's to be left to Jean when I pass. It has a false bottom. There is a key hidden in the headboard corner post of the matching bedroom set, also to be left to Jean. I'll show you the disguised keyhole when we return home. No one else alive knows of it, just you and me."

"Great. That'll do, Father. We'll decide later on what to do with Alex's treasure."

It was late afternoon when Thomas and the girls

returned. "Father," started Thomas, "we stopped at the O'Shey place, and Mr. O'Shey said to let you know Brad could and would help out."

"Thank you, Thomas. There have been some changes in plans. You and your sisters, join Grandfather and me. We'll eat at the O'Donnell boardinghouse this evening meal. Go in, and see what your mother would have us bring her for dinner, or perhaps she may want to join us," said Michael. As Thomas entered the house, Michael led his horse to the water trough and then took the grain sack from the buckboard to feed the animal.

Thomas joined the McNaire family at the front gate of Dr. Downs's. "Mother said she would eat later, Father," stated Thomas.

"All right then, let us go," jested Michael.

As the family sat at a table, Michael told Thomas, Susan, and Sharrie Lee they would spend the night at the O'Donnell boardinghouse. "After dinner, Thomas, bring the buckboard over, and unload your baggage. Susan, you and Sharrie take your mother a plate. She'll need to eat at some point. Then, Thomas, I want you to meet me at the White Horse at eight bells. You'll be staying to help the other clans round up stock and begin repairs on homesteads. Mind your manners. In the event we are not back come evening, you spend your nights at the farm."

"Yes, Father," answered the three McNaire children.

After dinner, the children did as they were directed. Grandfather and Michael walked the short distance to the White Horse Inn. The windows of the inn were boarded. A section of the roof toward the rear was pulled up. But it was still able to accommodate travelers, and the inn was conducting business as usual. As they entered the squeaking, swinging doors, they found a pleasant surprise. There at the long bar was Ken O'Shey, Brad's father. Michael and Grandfather took a schooner of ale with him. Michael filled him in on the updated plans he had made and thanked him anyway for his permission to let Brad help.

After the short stop, they headed back to the doctor's home. Michael told Jean of his intentions for the journey. As it was too late to start out that day, he and Grandfather were going back to the farm for the night. Jean was glad to hear that Michael was joining her for the trip to the hospital. Jean then bid her husband good night.

The two McNaire men made their way to the O'Donnell house. There, Michael ensured Sandy O'Donnell was paid. Sandy promised to get the children up and on their respected ways the next morning. Grandfather and his son made their way back home. When they arrived, it was still a decent time of day.

After Michael had brushed down his horse and put the tackle away, he entered the house. Grandfather showed Michael the hidden keyhole in the old cedar chest. Michael took the gold, put it in an old sock, secured it in the false bottom, and locked it up. Then Michael and Grandfather agreed to hide the key in its original place in the event one of them needed it and the other one was not around.

Throughout the third day, Alex remained motionless and silent.

CHAPTER 3
YORKSHIRE

The night passed quickly, and the McNaire farm was slowly beginning the day. Grandfather and Michael picked up some fruit for breakfast. Grandfather put on coffee while Michael fed the horse and prepared his rig for the journey. It was half past seven when they snapped the reigns and headed for the village. Thomas was already at the White Horse when they pulled up outside. It appeared that every clan had shown up, with men and older boys wall to wall. There was standing room only. Thomas made his way to Michael and told his father he would make him proud.

"Fine, Thomas," said Michael. "You do your part, and mind your manners, son. By the way, Thomas, I am already very proud to have you as my son."

"Thank you, Father," replied Thomas.

Thomas rejoined the others as Grandfather and Michael made their way to the O'Donnell house. Once there, Michael thanked Sandy O'Donnell and repacked the belongings Thomas had unloaded. The next stop was Dr. Downs's. When the buckboard reached the fence of Dr. Downs's, they pulled up beside a hospital wagon. Alex and Jean were already in the back and ready for the trip. Dr. Downs stood on the porch as Grandfather joined Jean in the back of the lead wagon. Susan and Sharrie Lee joined Michael on the seat of the buckboard.

The doctor called to Michael. "Jean has my reports. Godspeed, and may the wind be at your back." Michael waved as the wagons pulled out onto the main street. It was not too long before they left sight of the town.

Susan crawled over the seat into the back of the buckboard. Sharrie Lee placed her head on Michael's lap and snuggled into the seat. Soon, both girls were fast asleep. Michael tried to enjoy the view of the countryside. He found it hard not to think of Alex, the gold, and the state of his farm.

There were two cots in the back of the hospital wagon—Alex, of course, lay in one, and Jean sat on the edge of the other. Grandfather McNaire sat on a wooden bench alongside Alex's cot. An hour out of town, Grandfather encouraged Jean to lie down on her cot. He assured her he would wake her if there was any change in Alex. It did not take much coaching before Jean, too, was fast asleep.

As the day passed, Grandfather began to nod off until at last sleep overcame him. He slept until he began to feel a thumbing on his knee. He slowly came around to find Alex talking almost at a whisper. His foot was hitting Grandfather's knee. Alex had his eyes closed. He was talking in sentences, which seemed a good sign to Grandfather. He was about to wake up Jean but thought better of it. He put his ear close to Alex. The lad was calling out names Grandfather had never heard. With trembling in his soft words, Alex went on about giant spiders and things called Trogglites. Grandfather distinctly made out the names Brock, Leappy, and Yota. This went on for only a few moments. Then Alex went silent again. *Should I wake Jean?* thought Grandfather. No, she would be mad that he had not awakened her earlier. Grandfather was unable to fall back to sleep.

The small convoy pulled off the road to rest the animals for a spell. They stopped next to a cool stream and a few shade trees. The McNaires spread out a blanket and prepared a quick lunch. The driver of the covered wagon and Michael unhitched the horses and led them to the stream. Susan brought out a picnic basket prepared by Mrs. O'Donnell and sat it on the blanket. Jean was the last one awake after everything was in place. She looked down at Alex as her eyes watered.

"Mom's here, Alex. Please come back to us," Jean said. Then Grandfather helped her step down the tailgate stairs and walked her to the blanket under a large shade tree.

Michael and the driver joined the family after putting the feedbags on the horses. There was very little talk while they ate. Only the driver spoke. "It is yet several hours before we reach Yorkshire. It will be almost dusk by the time we arrive. However, we are making good time," ended the driver.

After lunch, Grandfather went to the stream, pulled out Alex's handkerchief, and dampened it with cool water. After he had placed it on Alex's forehead, he joined Michael for a pipe. The driver hitched the horses to both wagons as the girls cleaned up around the shade tree.

"Grandfather," began Michael, "how are Alex and Jean?"

"They both slept up to this point, son," answered

Grandfather. He thought it best not to mention Alex mumbling, and Alex did remain asleep.

The girls had put the picnic things in the back of the buckboard, and Jean yelled for the McNaire men to hurry along. Michael took his seat on the rig. Grandfather seated Jean and pulled the stairs back into the tailgate and then settled himself. With a short snap of the whip, the covered wagon pulled out, followed by Michael and the girls. As they rolled down the road, Jean took out a cold jug of water and a washcloth, poured the jug into the cloth, and began to wipe Alex's brow. Grandfather nearly stumbled from his seat. The damp handkerchief he had placed on Alex had vanished. He looked for it under the cot, to his left, and then to his right.

"Are you okay?" asked Jean.

"Yes, yes, I'm fine. It seems I've dropped me matches," said Grandfather. Knowing Jean could not see from the other side of the wagon, he bent down and then back up, putting his hands in his coveralls, saying, "Ah, here they be." Grandfather McNaire was old but of very sound mind. He knew he had placed the handkerchief on Alex's head, yet he could not explain where it had gone. Alex was in the wagon alone, and he knew he could not disturb the lad and search any further. He put the event out of his mind and began to fall asleep.

"Here, Father, change places with me, and catch a few winks," said Jean.

"Thanks. I could use a rest," said Grandfather.

Grandfather slept until he was awakened by voices. It seemed they had arrived in the large town of Yorkshire. People were active on both sides of the wagon. He looked out the rear of the wagon and could hardly believe his eyes. Grandfather was in his eighties and had never ventured far from the McNaire farm. The Blue Mountains were a fair journey but nothing like a city he had ever seen. There were streetlamps being lit by long poles up and down both sides of the street.

After they had made turns down several streets, they pulled up at the emergency entrance to the Yorkshire Hospital. Two male nurses pulling a cart on wheels hurried to the back end of the wagon. "Please step down," one of the nurses said to Grandfather and Jean. After Jean and Grandfather unboarded the wagon, the two nurses loaded Alex onto the rolling cart. Then they hurried him into the hospital. Jean was right on their heels.

"Catch up to your mother, girls," instructed Michael. "Let's find a livery stable and a hotel, father."

"Sure, son," answered Grandfather McNaire. They found the hotel first to unload the buckboard. They took three rooms at the hotel: one for Grandfather, one for the girls, and another for Michael and Jean. They dropped off the rig at the livery, and Michael paid for two days' feeding and storage. The two men made their way back to the hospital. Jean and the girls were in the main admitting room.

"Grandfather, why don't you and the girls eat dinner at the hotel? Then get some sleep. Jean and I will wait until Alex is settled in and then come along later," Michael said.

"Okay, girls, let's go see the lights of the town," said Grandfather.

After they arrived at the hotel, the threesome ate dinner. Then Grandfather took the two girls to their room and told them good night and that he would check in on them in a short while. Grandfather made his way back to the main lobby and the hotel pub for a schooner of ale. Actually, he drank three or four schooners. Even though a wee bit tipsy, he looked in on the girls. They were sound asleep. He then went to his quarters for the night. After taking off his boots, he propped up a pillow just for a short nap but soon feel into a deep sleep.

Michael escorted Jean back to their room. "Jean, I'll

sit with Alex till dawn. Then you come relieve me after you've eaten some breakfast. I'll eat when I come back," said Michael.

"Okay, dear," answered Jean.

Michael went back to the hospital as his wife retired for a much-needed rest. When Michael arrived in Alex's room, the nurse pulled up an easy chair for him.

"Would you like something to read or anything to eat, sir?" asked the nurse.

"No, no, thank you, I'll be fine," Michael said. "How's my lad?"

"We've bathed him and made him as comfortable as we can with a fresh gown. The doctors will be in to see him in the morning. Then we should know more. Good evening to you, sir," ended the nurse as she left the room.

Michael just gazed at Alex. The journey's wear on him began to sink in. He could barely keep his eyes open, but he managed to stay awake until the sun began to rise.

CHAPTER 4
UNANNOUNCED VISITOR

As Grandfather drifted off to sleep, he heard the town crier announce twenty-three bells (11:00 p.m.). It was very early in the morning when there came a tapping noise. This brought the old man around. Half-awake, Grandfather said, "Who is it?" There came no answer, so he asked again, "Who is there at me door?" Still no answer came. Then again came *tap-tap-tap*. *Blarney,* thought the old man as he started to rise up.

Then he heard a wee voice say, "Stay as you are, please." Grandfather looked about the room but did not see anyone. "Down here," said the voice, followed by *tap-tap-tap*. In the pale light of the streetlamps, Grandfather spotted a small figure sitting on the edge of the footboard of his bed, the same place the tapping had come from.

Not a large mouse, thought Grandfather. *It talks.* "Who is there?" he asked.

"Don't be frightened, sir. You're not dreaming," replied the voice. "If it is a name you need, you may call me Roe." The old man, still frozen in place, could but stare at the vague shadow. "Do not move too quickly, sir, or I will be off and gone before you reach this far," said Roe.

"Here, what are you that could be so small yet talk?"

"Well, Mr. McNaire—" said Roe.

"How do you know me name?" interrupted Grandfather.

"Never mind. I've been told to be extra polite and put you at ease as soon as possible. So that is what I'm trying to do," said Roe. "I'll talk; you listen. Okay, Mr. McNaire?"

"But—" started the old man.

"No buts, sir. No questions. Nothing at all. I talk; you listen. Agreed?" asked Roe.

"Agreed," grumbled the old man.

"First, outside of you and me, this visit never happened, unless you want your kinfolk to think you've lost your mind. Agreed?" asked Roe.

"Of course. I'm beginning to believe I already have," Grandfather McNaire said.

"Alex has been on a great adventure. Of this adventure

are details that must be kept from all humankind," began Roe. "It is only because Alex spoke of you that I now speak to you at all. You will have several questions, I am sure, most of which will go unanswered. Alex has knowledge of matters no other human has, most of which must remain with Alex. Alex may mumble of some strange places and odd things in the next few days. Such things will be dismissed as illusions or confusion. However, now, listen to every word I am about to tell you," stated Roe. "After Alex regains consciousness, he may mention certain names, places, and events, all of which happened to him—"

"You sound awfully sure of Alex's recovery," interrupted Grandfather.

"I am sure," Roe began. "Any further interruptions on your part may place Alex in some very unwelcome circumstances," snapped Roe.

"I am truly sorry. Please continue," Grandfather stated.

Roe began again. "It is now three bells. Alex will wake between nine and ten bells the day after tomorrow. It is urgent that you be nearby. Tell Alex these words: Anton is safe; hold your tongue. You must, Mr. McNaire, see that Alex does not speak of Anton at all. He may speak to you some when he is released from the hospital. It must appear that a bump on the head befell the lad and he was in a short coma and nothing more. Do you understand, sir?" asked Roe.

"Yes, I understand," replied Grandfather.

"For this service, you may ask one question of me," said Roe.

"The gold?" inquired Grandfather.

"It is in your best interest to keep silent about Alex's reward. You did not find it bound neatly in a handkerchief—this handkerchief, to be exact." Roe pulled out Alex's handkerchief and showed it to Grandfather.

"How …" began the old man.

"Stop, sir," said Roe. "One question only. Let me finish what I was telling you. It is possible that the tree was a hiding place in its younger days—that the gold was placed there by someone who was unable to retrieve it. As years passed, the tree grew around it. The splitting of the tree revealed the gold after years that it had been out of anyone's mind. This or some similar story would work. I'm sure you have landownership and mineral rights for your property. Regardless of your story, make it believable. The treasure still, by all rights, belongs to Alex. It must remain Alex's to do with as he sees fit. You, sir, will never see me again, nor did this meeting ever take place. Alex must not ramble on, or he will be placed in an institution—a terrible waste of his life. Make it clear to him not to speak of things he cannot prove. Understood?" finished Roe.

"Understood, whoever and whatever you are," agreed Grandfather.

"To ease your mind, Alex will return to you sound in mind and in body all at the appointed time. He was given a sleep potion to keep him asleep until the time came to contact you. So be assured your grandson is safe and pretty much unharmed. Do not look for me ever, for it will be impossible for you to find me. Alex will hear from us from time to time. Some things he may talk to you about as permission is granted. Other than this, do not quiz the lad. With that, sir, I bid you farewell," ended Roe.

In an instant, he was gone. Grandfather, now fully awake, pondered the events that had just taken place. He concluded that this meant at least some of the tales he had heard about the wee people (leprechauns) were indeed true. Also, he knew that he needed to follow through on what Roe asked of him. He spent the rest of the night in an uneasy sleep. The rest of the night passed easily for the other McNaires. Only Michael drifted in and out of sleep. He continually checked on Alex's condition. The nurse came in and out on every hour, which helped.

CHAPTER 5
MYSTERIOUS RESULTS

Grandfather, the girls, and Jean awakened at six bells. They prepared for the day and met in the hotel lobby café. After breakfast, they walked to the hospital. Michael had been brought a breakfast tray and had already finished eating when the rest of the family arrived in Alex's room.

"How was your night, Michael?" asked Jean.

"Fine, love," answered Michael. "Alex would make a few sounds and then stop on and off throughout the night. I couldn't make any sense out of what he mumbled. Of course, I'm so tired I wouldn't make much sense out of what anyone said now."

"You get some sleep," directed Jean.

"That I shall," replied Michael. "Take a pipe, Father?" he asked.

"Sure, son, let's go," answered Grandfather.

The female McNaires gathered around Alex's bed. They began talking about the large city as they looked over Alex. Grandfather and Michael puffed on their pipes and exchanged but a few passing words. Then Michael left for the hotel and bed. Grandfather returned to Alex's room. As he entered, so did a doctor and nurse.

"My name is Dr. Henderson," said the doctor to Jean. "I'm ordering some x-rays and tests to run on your son. If you have anything you'd like to do, feel free. The tests and all will take a few hours. See our beautiful city if you choose. There is a lot to be seen here."

Susan and Sharrie Lee asked Jean, "Could we, Mother? Could we, please?"

"Of course we can," said Jean. "Alex is in good hands, and I am a bit tired of sitting. Grandfather, will you be joining us?"

"I believe I'll wait around here, Jean," said Grandfather McNaire.

"All right then, let us see Yorkshire, girls. We will be back, Father, or better yet, why don't we meet up with you? We'll meet you in the cafeteria around noon," finished Jean.

"That will be fine, Jean," said Grandfather.

The elderly man sat in the easy chair next to Alex's bed. He bent over and whispered in Alex's ear, "Anton is safe; hold your tongue." He repeated the sentence twice and then settled back in the easy chair. Grandfather drifted off to sleep. He did not notice the orderlies take Alex down the long hallway for x-rays even when they brought Alex back. The nurse also came in and took some blood tests without disturbing Mr. McNaire at all.

When the old man came around, he was still alone with Alex. He stretched his arms and let out a yawn. "Now there, Alex," started Grandfather McNaire, "there seems to be more to your story than meets the eye, lad. You are going to be just fine. I can hardly wait to talk to you."

The doctor entered the room and inquired as to the whereabouts of Michael and Jean. Grandfather explained that Michael was catching some sleep and the girls were in Yorkshire.

"Could you round them up for me, sir? I have some words on Alex for them," said the doctor.

"Sure, I can," stated the old man. "I'm meeting Jean in the cafeteria at noon. I'll send Susan for Michael."

"Thank you. There is no hurry; just an update on Alex," replied the doctor.

After lunch with the girls, Grandfather sent Susan for Michael. They all met up back in Alex's room. When the doctor came in, Jean braced herself against Michael's shoulder.

"You can ease up, miss," said the doctor. "Alex's x-rays verify he has no broken bones or bleeding inside. However, I have found something unusual in Alex's blood samples. It seems to be organic by nature. It is nothing like I have ever seen before. I've sent samples to the lab for a more expert opinion. I should have the results in an hour or so. Until then, all we can do for Alex is wait," he concluded.

The McNaire family settled themselves around Alex's bed. Michael and Grandfather first stepped out for a pipe. The female McNaires began a conversation on their brief tour of the town. The time flew by quickly, and the family once again bunched around the doctor.

"It is very strange indeed. After the lab sent back their findings, which they found normal, I took another look and found nothing wrong either. I'm ordering another sample to be drawn. I wish to take another look," said the doctor. The nurse came in and drew another vile of Alex's blood and hurried off.

The McNaires began a conversation and gathered around Alex.

"Alex will be just fine," stated Grandfather.

"Yes, I am sure he will pull through and be the same young lad we all know," said Michael.

"I'm still deeply concerned," said Jean.

The girls just sighed and said, "Yes, we understand, Mother."

There was a period of silence before the doctor came back in. "I still don't believe it," said the doctor.

"Believe what?" asked Jean.

"Right before my own eyes," continued the doctor as he stared at Alex.

"What is just before your eyes?" asked Jean.

"Alex's blood contains some very unusual chemical. First it is there, and then it is gone. Not a very professional explanation, but that is what happened. Did Alex drink or eat anything out of the ordinary the past few days?" asked the doctor.

"No," answered Jean in a questioning tone. Then Michael explained the storm and the way they had found Alex.

"I see," replied the doctor. "I want to run tests on the lad every six hours. Perhaps it may help me understand what's happening and if it has anything or nothing to do with Alex being in a coma."

"Whatever you think is best for Alex, Doctor. It's getting to be late afternoon," said Michael. "Why don't we all eat an early dinner as a family and discuss some matters of concern?"

When the McNaires were seated and their dinner ordered, Michael began to speak. "I was planning on leaving early in the morning. I believe I'll wait around and see what is determined with Alex and his test."

"Thanks for staying, Michael," said Jean. "This whole storm, home, and Alex thing has me a bit shaken. I hope Thomas is doing all right and that they have found our stock. I wouldn't know what to do for meals without milk, butter, cream, eggs, and chickens—"

"Stop that, Jean," interrupted Michael. "We will be just fine. Please, I've provided for you always and will continue to do so. You must not spread yourself so thin. It's hard on your heart and health. Please, Jean, calm down a bit. Perhaps a short nap would help."

"Perhaps just a short nap would help," Jean repeated.

"Sharrie Lee and Susan, what would you like to do?" asked Michael.

"A little nap would be good," said Susan.

"Me too, Father. I will take a nap also," added Sharrie Lee.

"Fine then," finished Michael.

"Let's take a pipe, son," said Grandfather. The two men stepped outdoors.

"Michael, after I finish me pipe, I'll lie down for a while. You can sit with Jean for a stretch tonight with Alex. I'll relieve you for the late shift. How would that be?" asked Grandfather.

"That would be very kind of you, Papa. Father, you seem to be quieter than usual," said Michael.

"Yes, son, I am pondering a lot of things today. Mostly Alex. These tests have me concerned too. As your mother would say, it'll all come out in the wash. I truly believe it will," ended Grandfather.

CHAPTER 6

ANOTHER RUDE AWAKENING

Jean and Michael sat at Alex's bedside. They spoke of the farm and of Susan's wedding Susan being the oldest of the Mcnaire children at 17 was arranged to be wed to Brad O'Shey, the following spring. Then came Thomas two years younger, Alex at 15 the youngest son and Sherrie Lee at age 5 was the youngest. Sleep was trying to win them over. They managed to stay awake. Jean rubbed her eyes and then stared at Alex. She swore to Michael she had seen Alex move a foot. "May be a reflex," said Michael as he, too, began to stare at Alex. Then, without a doubt, Alex lifted a hand. Jean yelled out for the nurse.

The nurse was quick to respond. She adjusted Alex's pillow as she asked, "What's the problem, Mrs. McNaire?"

"Alex moved. He moved." Jean repeated herself.

"Well, let's see," the nurse said.

As they watched and watched, nothing happened. The nurse looked at Jean, then at Alex. She was about to look back to Jean when Alex lifted both hands and wiggled his right foot. "Looks like very good news," said the nurse. "He still has a little way to come back yet. These are very good signs that he is doing just that. I'll send the news to the doctor, who has gone home for the night. He will probably want me to observe through the remainder of the night in the event a further development occurs. He would then come in. Alex could continue like this for hours or longer and get more active or even drift backward. We'll have to wait and see. All in all, it is wonderful for you to see the healing has begun. I'm very happy for you," finished the nurse.

Hours had passed since the last time Alex had moved when Grandfather McNaire showed up to relieve Jean and Michael. After telling Grandfather about the good news, they made him promise to come for them if anything at all happened.

"As quick as I can, Jean. As quick as I can," Grandfather finished.

After Michael and Jean left, Grandfather sat down in the easy chair next to Alex. He whispered in the lad's ear, "Anton is safe; hold your tongue." Then Grandfather sat back in the easy chair and stared at Alex intently. He stepped out from time to time to smoke his pipe. "Anytime now, Alex. Anytime," he repeated to himself.

It was around eight bells and the sun was already rising when Grandfather was brought out of a half-asleep state by Alex tugging on his shirtsleeve. "Alex," said Grandfather.

Alex just stared in disbelief at the old man. "Where am I, Grandfather, and where are Leappy and the others?" questioned Alex.

"Listen, Alex, all I can tell you is Anton is safe and you are to hold your tongue on that subject. Some small creature named Roe told me to tell you that and that you would understand," Grandfather said.

"Yes, but how did I get here?" Alex asked.

"Son, we found you by your nap tree in the fields. Alex, there are a lot of questions I have for you too. I've been told by Roe, the little creature, not to ask," Grandfather stated.

"If you could only believe, Grandfather—then again, I'm having a terrible time believing some things myself," Alex said.

"In any case, Alex, you must not go on about Anton

in front of others until Roe talks to you, which Roe did say he would do later. It's for your own good to act like the storm was to blame for an awful bump on your head and it put you in a coma, lest they put you away for losing your mind. I'm not sure of what all that means. However, that is what I've been told to tell you," finished Grandfather.

"I can understand more than you think, Grandfather. I've listened to my new friends enough to know I must do as I'm told in regard to Anton and all," Alex said

"All what?" Grandfather asked.

"I'll tell you what I'm told I can tell you as soon as I know what that is, Grandfather," said Alex.

"I guess that will have to do, Alex, but there are a few things you will have to explain." Grandfather was about to tell Alex about the gold when Jean, Michael, and the girls walked into the room.

"Alex!" screamed Jean.

"Are you all right, son?" asked Michael.

"I am a bit hungry. My head aches a little bit, but that's about it," Alex said.

"Thank God," said Jean.

The nurse entered and was pleasantly surprised to see Alex sitting up and talking. "Welcome back, Alex," said the nurse.

"Thank you," answered Alex.

"The doctor will be pleased to see you're awake. How do you feel?" asked the nurse.

"Hungry," Alex said.

"We will take care of that after I give you a quick check," remarked the nurse. The nurse checked Alex's temperature, pulse, and blood pressure. "Fit as a fiddle you are. Now, I'll have some breakfast sent in."

The family sat down and told Alex all about the storm and how they found him. "A miracle," Jean said.

"Yes, it is good to have you back with us. Ya had me worried, son. I mean, who would do all your work?" Michael said with a smile, just joking with Alex.

The doctor stepped into the room, also with a smile. "Ah, what a wonderful physician I am. I knew I could bring you through." He said this in a joking manner. "Now that you're awake, lad, can you tell me if you have aches or pain anywhere?"

"Just a wee headache," Alex answered the doctor.

"That is to be expected," said the doctor. "Still, I want to run some blood samples and keep you another twenty-four hours before we consider sending you home. I'll order the tests; then we will see."

"All right, Doc," Alex jested.

The McNaires openly spoke about how good it was to have Alex recover in such good health. Only Grandfather knew that it was not a miracle—that Alex had been fine all along.

After a few hours, the doctor came back in with a puzzled look. "It seems that all traces of that strange chemical have vanished. Quite a mystery to me. All in all, you can make arrangements for Alex to be released tomorrow morning. I'd appreciate a letter now and then letting me know of any changes in Alex and how he is doing," the doctor concluded.

"Sure, we will let you know, and thank you, Doctor, for your concern," said Michael.

CHAPTER 7
HOME AT LAST

The day Alex awoke went by very quickly. The girls and Jean washed the laundry and hung it to dry and then repacked it for the trip home. Michael, Grandfather, and Alex spent most of the day talking about the farm. The gold came up once, and Alex could not explain how it had got in his handkerchief and in the tree—not even the one deplume he had held in his hand.

"It might come back to me later, Father, but for now, I just do not remember much after seeing the ball of lightning," stated Alex.

The truth was he did not know how the gold had ended up where it did or where it had come from. He did, however, recall his time in Anton and most of the events that took place. He recalled Princess Dora, Leappy, Yota,

Brock, Gordon, Jessica, Uncle Satchen, and others. He knew he had to keep those things to himself but found it hard to imagine what had really happened to him. Sometimes, it all seemed like a dream.

The family ate dinner with Alex in the cafeteria. "I can hardly wait to see home," Alex said.

"What is left of it," said Grandfather.

"Thomas and others from the village have been working at gathering stock and making the surrounding farms that survived the storm livable," said Michael.

"There will be plenty to do when we get back, I'm sure," said Grandfather.

"It will be just wonderful," Jean said. "We are all going home, and Alex too. Home will be home no matter the shape of things."

After dinner, Jean and Alex returned to Alex's room. The rest said good night to Alex and left for the hotel. After Alex settled into bed, Jean sat in the easy chair. "You get some rest, son. I'll be right here if you need anything," said Jean. "It will take most of tomorrow to get home."

"By the way, where are we, Mother?" asked Alex.

"Yorkshire," answered Jean.

"Never been here before," said Alex.

"Maybe we'll visit again, son, when things get a little

more normal," Jean finished. Little did she know things would never again be normal. The McNaire family was about to go through some big changes.

Michael and Grandfather were up early, and they ate before waking the girls. As the female McNaires sat down to breakfast, Michael and Grandfather left for the livery stables. They hitched up the buckboard and fed the horse. When they returned to the hotel, they loaded up the luggage. Susan, and Sharrie Lee were ready to leave at about the same time as the packing was finished. Then they all got aboard and headed for the hospital.

"It is a beautiful town," said Susan.

"Perhaps next spring, or sooner, we can come again" said Michael. "There is a lot of work, and there still may be a harvest. The storm did not hurt the potato crop any. In fact, it may have helped it a great deal. We will have to see."

Alex was dressed and ready to leave when his family arrived. After final words with the doctor and signing countless papers, they were able to fit everyone into the buckboard. They headed for the edge of town and the long road home. Alex looked the countryside over and was deep in thought about Princess Dora and how she yearned to see the sky and trees. He missed the company of Leappy but not the memory of the Battle of Clarion. Who would believe him even if he could talk about it?

Grandfather sat next to Alex. Susan and Sharrie Lee fell asleep as Michael and Jean rode in the front seat of the wagon. Remembering Roe's words, Grandfather didn't force Alex to talk about Anton, but he was making himself available to Alex should he decide to speak on the subject.

"Grandfather," asked Alex, "do you believe in the leprechauns? You tell us stories about the wee people. Where did you hear these stories?"

"Do I believe in leprechauns? Well, Alex, through the years, I've come to believe there is more to the stories than one could prove. As of the past few days, I am more inclined than ever before to say yes," Grandfather answered.

"They are real, Grandfather—as real as you and I," said Alex.

"Now, listen, Alex; your friend Roe told me you would want to talk and, when you did, it would be to me. Roe also warned me to let you know not to speak of your experiences in great detail until you've talked with him. Now, lad, I would love to hear your whole story, but I don't want you to place yourself in harm's way. I'm curious, yes, but I also believe the wee man was very serious when he spoke with me. There is the matter of the gold—" stated the old man.

"What gold?" Alex interrupted.

"When we found you, lad, you were holding a gold piece in your hand. Your brother, Thomas, found nineteen others in your handkerchief stuck in the split tree," said Grandfather.

"Where did it come from?" Alex asked.

"I was hoping you could answer that," Grandfather responded.

"No, sir, I truly don't know," said Alex.

"Well, perhaps it will come back to you, Alex; then again, maybe it won't. In either case, your father and I will come up with a story of how it ended up in your possession."

"*Mine*, Grandfather?" asked Alex.

"Of course yours. It was wrapped in your handkerchief, so it's clear you put it there, or it was put there intended for you," insisted Grandfather.

"Glory be," said Alex.

Michael pulled off the road at the same place they had eaten a few days earlier on the way to Yorkshire. After the family again had eaten, Jean, Susan, and Sharrie Lee cleaned up and repacked the picnic things. Grandfather and Michael leaned against the big tree and packed their pipes for a smoke. Alex walked down a small path that led to the stream. As he stared at his reflection in the water, his thoughts were clear and sharp. He pictured Anton and Princess Dora. *She would really love to see this place,* thought Alex. Alex was brought back to reality when he heard Michael's voice shout out his name.

Alex began his short walk back up the path, but he froze in his tracks. In the middle of the path lay his handkerchief folded nice and neat. On top of the hanky was a single gold deplume. Alex quickly picked up the small bundle and placed it deep in his pocket. He knew it was a sign that leprechauns were around. "Leappy," whispered Alex, "Leappy, if you can hear me, tell Princess Dora I am all right and hope all is well in Anton. I miss you also, my friend."

As Alex drew nearer to the buckboard, Michael looked at him, puzzled. "Were ya talking to yourself, son?" asked Michael.

"Just thinking out loud, Father," said Alex.

"I'll bet you had a lot to say, son, after all you've been through," jested Michael.

"Sure, Father, but everything will turn out just fine—at least that's what I choose to believe," Alex replied.

"That's very wise thinking, Alex. Maybe that bump on the head was just what you needed."

Alex thought, *If you only knew, Father. If you only knew the things I have seen.*

Once aboard the rig, the McNaires made their way down the dirt road toward the farm and their home. When the family arrived at the old farm, they were a bit taken aback. The corral gate and barn doors were hung back on their hinges. Even the nanny goat and chickens had been put back in their proper place.

It was early evening when Jean and the girls, assisted by Alex, unloaded the luggage and carried it into the house. *What a blessing,* thought Jean as she entered the newly hung kitchen screen door. It did not make a single squeak while opening or closing. Michael and Grandfather unhitched the horse and hung the tackle in the barn. The barn also was well organized and clean.

"Father," started Michael, "remind me to thank the squire and our neighbors. I'm forever in their debt."

"I don't believe they will look at things that way, Michael. It is the clansmen way to help out their neighbors.

Besides, you would have done things the same way had times been different," Grandfather responded.

"Yes, Father, of course, but I believe thanks are still in order just the same," said Michael. "Let's get settled back in and help Jean and the children put things back together in the house. Thomas should be home shortly. Tomorrow, I will help him and the others. While I'm gone, you can look around the place and see what's left to be done."

As Thomas rode up, he noticed chimney smoke. To him, this meant his family was home and his mother was cooking. *Great,* he thought, *after today's work, I am starving.* As Thomas entered the house, the family was sitting down at the dinner table.

"Wash up, Thomas. We're just starting dinner. You're just in time," Jean said. For the first time in days, the McNaires sat down for a meal as an entire family. Susan and Sharrie filled Thomas in on Yorkshire and their tour of the city. Thomas listened intently and was a little envious.

"Thomas, we may all be going back next spring. It depends on the crops, the winter, and Susan's wedding. You'll not begin to believe all the girls have told you, and there was much, much more that we ourselves did not see," Jean said.

"That would be fun, Mother. I look forward to

seeing it," began Thomas. "There has been a great deal of destruction in these parts. We've been working sunup till sundown. Some folks lost everything. Some stock are still missing or mixed in with others. I'm sure they will all end up in the right place in time. I'm pretty tired and looking forward to bed. Mr. Fletcher picks me up right as the cock crows," Thomas finished.

"You can retire as early as you want, son. I'll be joining you tomorrow," said Michael. "Thank you, son, for being of such help. You make me proud to be your father. I'm sure the more help we get, the better for all of us in these parts. I want to do my fair share."

"Me too, Papa, me too. I want to do my fair share and make you proud," Alex said.

"No," said Jean.

"What I think your mother means is it's a bit too soon, Alex. You still need rest. Besides, I am very proud of all my children. Not a better lot could a man ask for," said Michael.

"That is very sweet of you, Michael," said Jean. "Of course that's what I intended to say, Alex. We will see what the next few days bring. I am a very proud mother of four wonderful children—sometimes five, when Grandfather acts up."

"Thank you, Mother," said Grandfather McNaire with a chuckle, knowing Jean was looking for a rise out of him.

"Thomas, you lay your things out for tomorrow, say your prayers, and get your sleep. I'll take care of your chores. Sharrie, you help your mother, and Susan, you can help Alex with his chores if he is up to it," Michael said.

"I'll manage just fine," Alex jumped in.

"What's the matter, Alex? Don't want a girl to help?" Susan said.

"Sure, you can tag along, but I will manage. You'll see," said Alex.

After chores, Susan and Sharrie Lee sat in the living room sewing a new dress for Sharrie Lee's doll, Chelsie. Michael and Jean sat at the kitchen table talking.

Alex sat on the front porch looking at the stars. He remembered sitting with Princess Dora and describing the sights he was now observing. His stomach felt a little uneasy. His memories were so vivid, so true to life. He felt sorrow for his friends. He daydreamed about Anton and the time he spent there. Mostly he wondered about the war and the horrible enemy of Anton in regard to those he grew so fond of. His eyes began to tear up as he thought of his friend Brock being squeezed and tossed about by the giant spider. Then he could almost feel the pinchers of the other tarantula about his waist. How could it not have been real? How could he be here now? He almost began to cry. Then Jean called him in to retire for the night. Now the McNaires were all at home as a family once more.

CHAPTER 8

MESSAGE FOR ALEX

As the sun kissed the peaks of the Blue Mountains, the McNaire farm stirred to life. Michael and Thomas were both ready for work. Mr. Fletcher never bothered to dismount his horse when he bid the two good morning. Michael and Thomas mounted their horses, and the three rode off to meet the day.

After breakfast and the morning chores, Alex asked to visit his favorite spot under his nap tree. Grandfather said, "I'm heading into town, Alex. I'll walk with you as far as the fields. Then I'll cut through the tree lines to the White Horse Inn."

"Mother, may I?" asked Alex.

"If you feel up to it, son, but don't be awfully long, or I'll worry myself sick," Jean said.

"Thank you, Mother. I won't stay long. I'll be back by lunch," Alex responded.

"Okay, off, the two of you. Leave the work to us girls," jested Jean.

"I couldn't think of more capable hands." Grandfather smirked.

"Grandfather," started Alex, "show me where you found the gold."

"Sure, lad. When we get to your tree, I'll point it out to ya," said Grandfather.

The two of them made their way to the field and Alex's tree. There was not much of a tree left. They would eventually cut it up for firewood.

Once they arrived, Grandfather asked Alex if he remembered anything at all about the gold deplumes. "No, not yet, sir," said Alex. "Grandfather, there is a lot I do recall, most of which, even if I could tell it, would have you believe I was bonkers."

"Alex, me lad, I've been around a long time and heard a lot of things. After the other night and meeting Roe, it is possible we are both bonkers, which I refuse to believe, but I would not share the experience of that night with anyone other than you," Grandfather responded.

"I understand, Grandfather," said Alex.

"In any case, lad, this is where the gold bundled in your handkerchief lay when we first found you," Grandfather stated. He pointed to the spot in the tree.

Alex just scratched his head. *Nineteen pieces of gold plus one in my hand and one on me hanky on the path. Where did it all come from, and why is it all to be mine?* "Well, thank you, Grandfather. I'll be fine here. I'll see you this evening when you return home," said Alex.

"I'll see you then, Alex, but mind you are home for lunch, lest your mother come after ya, lad," finished Grandfather as he walked through the trees toward the village.

Alex stood by his tree and looked all around him. *What must have happened here?* He began to recall the cool breeze he felt after swimming in the stream. He walked over to the tree. It was ripped down the middle and charred black from the lightning. He looked all up and down it for any signs of holes or burrows, hoping to find out how he ended up underground. *How did I get back here from Anton?* Alex questioned himself.

"Ya won't find anything, you know," said a small voice. Alex looked around until his eyes fell on an outcrop of rocks. It was a leprechaun, not any leprechaun he knew. "Have some questions, do ya, lad?" asked the wee person.

"Ay," said Alex. "First off, who might you be?" Alex asked.

"My name is Roe. I am an envoy to the king of Anton sent to you by order of Princess Dora."

"That answers that question," Alex said. "How are things with the princess and the king?"

"As well as one might expect at times like these. That is, as times are in Anton," said Roe.

"What may times be like in that kingdom?" Alex quizzed Roe.

"Alex, I will tell you what I can, because my knowledge of war is limited. First, this message from the princess may ease your mind. Then again, it may cause you great concern," said Roe.

"Come out with it then, Roe. What is it the princess has to tell me?" snapped Alex.

"She feels you would want to know of your reward—"

"Yes, I do," Alex interrupted.

"Alex, your kind tell tales of leprechauns and pots of gold. A few of those tales are not farfetched. How they became the knowledge of your people is a mystery—a mystery pondered through timeless ages. The pots of gold are real, all right. They are sacred and cherished among folk such as me. Upon the birth of an Elwarf or Dwarelf, a pot of steel is forged and stamped with the name of the newborn. Each year that passes in that lifetime, one gold deplume is forged and cast to put into the pot. They are to reflect the joy of life to my people. So a leprechaun's gold belongs only to that individual.

"At life's end—a very long time in your years, up in the hundreds in mine—the gold deplumes are melted down and made into a vessel. This vessel carries the remains of my kind upon a barge. The barge is then lowered into the River of No Return just south of the city of Urbane. Then it is left to float with the flow of the river. It is never seen again. There are many tales and thoughts on where the river leads to. Many have tried to find out, only to follow that river into a mist from which no seeker has ever returned. You were given your first directly from Princess Dora, then nineteen when you were brought back where you stand now. I left your twenty-first one on the path for you to find, which you did."

"I see," said Alex. "But I'm not a leprechaun, and I'm only fifteen years of age."

"True," said Roe. "The king of Anton gave you three: two of his and one from Dora. Then each of the knights to the king in each satellite city furnished three. Six cities plus Anton makes seven times three each, equaling twenty-one for your service to our kingdom and for the valor you showed in your willingness to give your own life in battle for our cause. It is said that even our most prized possession is not enough to show our gratitude to you," Roe finished.

"Leappy?" asked Alex.

"I am afraid I don't know of anyone named Leappy," said Roe.

"Yota," said Alex.

"Oh yes, Yota is very well known by all. Last I heard, he was still with his troops in the badlands south of Clarion. I'm sorry; that is all I know, except the war is still not won. Perhaps as I visit from time to time, I'll have more news. Until then, you may tell your grandfather you have spoken with me. Not any of what I told you today are you to mention—only the part about the gold being given to you as a reward for your help. Tell him none of the folklore you've heard. Only tell him things of Anton he may find entertaining. Like the rivers we use for travel, the waterfalls and such. Nothing about the Court of Royal children or the counsel of Chevrons. He is not to look for us. You know as well as I that he could not find anything unless you told him, which would not be wise. In the meantime, Alex, be safe, and live to be very old. Best wishes to you, and spend your reward wisely. There is one last thing Princess Dora told me in private: she misses you deeply and you are forever on her mind. Now, are there any words you would like me to take back to Anton?" Roe asked.

"Yes, send word to Yota all goes well with me, and make sure Leappy hears the same. In private, tell Princess Dora I, too, miss her and will never forget her. Thank you, Roe. Do you know when I will see you again?"

"No," responded Roe, "I assure you it will be quite often, as it is my duty to watch how you fare. You'll know I am around when you need to know."

"As you say, Roe, may the love of your queen Aurelie, be with you," said Alex.

"Alex, just turn around slowly one time. Again, I bid you farewell," said Roe.

Alex did as he was told. Once he finished a complete circle and again looked at the outcrop of rocks, Roe had vanished. *Gee,* thought Alex, *I wonder how they do that.*

Alex picked up a few smooth stones and skipped them across the stream as he pondered what he would or would not tell Grandfather McNaire. It was getting close to noon when Alex began his stroll back to the farmhouse.

CHAPTER 9
RETURN TO YORKSHIRE

Alex could barely wait for Grandfather McNaire to return home. Susan and Sharrie Lee were preparing the evening meal. Jean was setting the table under the old elderberry tree. It was the McNaires' night to dine outside, as was their custom once a week—weather permitting, of course.

Alex sat on the front porch and watched the horizon. He could see mounted horses approaching the farm. Then came a much-missed sound; he heard Grandfather coming up the path singing a jolly old Irish jingle. He was weaving back and forth as he neared the house. Grandfather bid Alex hello as he sat down on the steps of the front porch.

"Hello to you also," Alex said. "Father and Thomas are almost home. I have some good news to share with you after dinner, Grandfather. I've seen Roe today and can tell you some things you might not believe."

"That's great, Alex. I could use a little good news right about now. What about the gold?" Grandfather questioned.

"It's mine, all right, and I'll explain later when we are alone," said Alex.

Michael and Thomas rode in and dismounted. "Thomas, take the horses to the barn. Just unsaddle them for now. We'll brush them down and feed them after dinner," Michael said.

"Okay, Papa," answered Thomas as he led the horses to the barn.

"Wash up for dinner, everyone!" yelled Jean.

Susan and Sharrie brought the last of the meal out to the table. Michael told his family of his day in the countryside and of some neighbors who lost their homes to the storm. A few needed to be torn down and rebuilt. Grandfather added some news of a few other small communities that had been hit hard by the past week's storm. The news came from travelers stopping at the inn.

At dinner's end, Michael and Thomas headed for the barn. The girls and Jean cleared the table.

Grandfather and Alex took a short walk. As they strolled through the McNaire farm property, Alex began to tell Grandfather his version of where he had been from the time he woke up underground. He left out the parts that would reveal the magic and secrets of Anton. When he had finished telling Grandfather the leprechaun legacy, Grandfather was truly in disbelief. "Alex, you mean there are hundreds, maybe thousands, of wee people under our feet right now?" asked Grandfather.

"Clarion, the city where I first woke up, was destroyed by the lightning, myself, and floodwaters. Anton, the capital city, was three days' trip from there. To tell you the truth, I don't even know in what direction we went underground. The story of Aurelie and the crown of seven crystals should explain to you how leprechauns came to be—that is, if you can believe," said Alex.

"I believe because I have been there and lived among the wee people and grown quite fond of a few of them. Quite a tale, Alex," said Grandfather.

"The war I spoke of with you was still in the heat of battle against Trogg and Coret, two evil brothers who wish to destroy Anton. They want the main crystal that sits atop the Tower of Anton so as to control the kingdom. If they were to succeed, it would be a tragic event indeed.

Roe had little information on the subject of war. The gold was left as a reward for my services. How I ended up back aboveground where you found me is a mystery. Perhaps someday I'll learn the how and why of it all. Here I am, and we must decide what the best use of the reward would be. I have a few ideas but want to wait for you and Father to formulate your story as to how it came to be our property," Alex said.

"I think it best to take care of matters at hand and let the subject of gold rest a bit. Don't you, Alex?" asked Grandfather.

"Sure, I think that best also," Alex agreed.

The next few weeks became a routine for the McNaire men, working on rebuilding their home and helping their neighbors. After the last farmhouse was completed and the family moved back in, they still had to do the harvest before fall turned into winter.

Though Alex visited the tree by the fields often, he never saw Roe. When his full strength and health returned, he jumped straight into helping his father and Thomas in the fields. School also started for Alex. He was often caught daydreaming. His teachers sent home notes with him to Michael and Jean. Michael had more than one talk with Alex on the matter. As hard as he tried, Alex found it hard not to think of Anton and his friends.

It came time for Michael to visit the county seat to inquire about the deeds to the farm. "Mr. McTavish, am I reading this deed correctly, where it says I own all rights to the property?" Michael asked.

"Yes, Michael," Mr. McTavish, the county registrar of deeds, stated.

"What if I was to discover things buried in my land or found among my trees?" asked Michael.

"Well, Michael, anything you might find would be yours, provided no one else claimed to have lost it on your property. If that were to happen, they must claim it within thirty days or forfeit it to you."

"Well, thank you, Mr. McTavish. I need to make arrangements to visit Yorkshire," said Michael. "I'll explain more when I return. Can you draw up copies of my deeds and mineral rights, Mr. McTavish? I'll return in a few hours for them."

"Sure, Mr. McNaire. Did ya hit an oil pocket or something?" the assessor asked.

"No," began Michael, "something much better than that. For now, just the papers, please, proving I own my property."

"Very well, very well. As you say, McNaire, two hours," McTavish said.

Then Michael made his way to the White Horse Inn to meet with Grandfather McNaire. As Michael walked down the board-planked sidewalk, he noticed the chill in the air. He felt thankful that the harvest was nearly complete even in the hard times of Ireland. Most of his crop was sold and enough left for quartering to be placed in the barn to eye sprout for next year's crop. He then chuckled to himself, thinking, *That is, if I plant next year. The McNaires are rich.*

Once he entered the swinging doors of the White Horse—which also did not squeak anymore—he joined Grandfather and the squire at a table. After a short time of idle conversation, the squire had business to attend to. The squire excused himself from the table, leaving just Michael and Grandfather McNaire. After ordering two schooners of ale, they began to talk.

"Father, Mr. McTavish has assured me anything found on our property is ours, provided what was found is naturally part of the earth or natural in matter. Any material items that are unclaimed for thirty days become ours. I would venture the gold to be older than thirty days," Michael stated.

"Son, it's many times older in itself. I couldn't guess how long it's been in that tree," said Grandfather McNaire.

"Whatever does that mean, Father?" asked Michael.

"Well, Michael, I don't believe the gold has always been there, though I can't explain where it did come from," Grandfather responded.

"That's all well and good. It has been more than thirty days since we found it there," snapped Michael.

"Sure, son," began Grandfather McNaire, "it is Alex's property free and clear. We can't just sell it with that story of being found in a tree in a fairly new hanky."

"True enough," said Michael.

Grandfather remembered Roe's words from his short visit that night. "Suppose, Michael, a long time ago, pirates or thieves planted the gold in a much younger tree. Whoever planted it there was unable to retrieve it. The tree grew right around the gold in an old burlap bag that rotted away and allowed the coins to separate. After the lightning struck, we dug them out."

"I don't know how you came about such a tale. However, it sounds like it just might work," said Michael. "Of course, we need to cover these things with Alex."

"Of course," agreed Grandfather.

"After school and dinner, we will make time to talk

to the lad. Until then, I have to check the prices at the mercantile and pick up the copies of our deeds. You can stay put and enjoy your chess game and your friends. You've earned the right, Father, to enjoy your retirement years," Michael said.

"Thank you, son. I will, and I fully agree. I ran that farm too many years with you and your three sisters and dear, sweet mother. I'll see you tonight," said Grandfather McNaire.

Alex was finishing up his homework assignment when Michael arrived home from the village. Susan was at the O'Sheys' home, Jean and Sharrie Lee were hanging laundry to dry, and Thomas was quartering potatoes in the barn. All Michael let Alex know was that the gold was his and to start giving some serious thought to its uses.

Susan met Grandfather on the road to the McNaire farm. They walked home together.

"Are you getting the jitters about spring coming, Susan?" asked Grandfather.

"Not too much, Grandfather. It's still a few months away yet. I suppose I am a little anxious," Susan replied.

When Susan and Grandfather arrived home, Susan went to the kitchen to prepare dinner. She was soon joined by Jean and Sharrie Lee. Grandfather and Michael stepped out for a pipe. Thomas left the barn to wash up and change his clothes. Potatoes at that time of year had plenty of juice, and when they were cut, the juice would run all down his arms.

Alex was lost in thought over the gold, and he all but forgot his homework. He was failing at school. He was an eleventh grader and barely had passed the year before. He struggled through his math assignment and then slammed the book closed. *Finished,* he thought just as dinner was called. He joined the others at the kitchen table.

After saying grace, back-and-forth conversation began. Alex just waited for breaks in the talk to ask for things to be passed to him. Once his plate was full, he just moved his food about the plate, hardly eating anything. He was daydreaming again. He had so many things to do with his reward he couldn't remember them all. Jean told him to come back to earth and eat. He tried his best to obey her, but it wasn't at all easy for him.

"Jean, after dinner, Alex, Grandfather, and I are going to have a small meeting about school, chores, and such," said Michael.

"Sure, Mr. McNaire, if it is my approval you need, you have it," Jean said.

Grandfather and Alex sat on the front porch swing as Michael buttoned up his winter jacket. "Getting mighty cool this evening," said Michael.

"Yes, it won't be long before the trees start losing their leaves. Well, Alex, would you like to see your reward?" Grandfather asked.

"Could I? I mean, yes, of course," Alex said.

"I'll wait out here," Michael said.

Alex and Grandfather McNaire entered the house and went to the old man's room. Grandfather went to the headboard and removed the top of the corner bedpost. "What in the name of Saint Peter?" gasped Grandfather. "It's gone!"

"What's gone, Grandfather?" Alex asked.

"My key," said Grandfather. "But where?"

"How about over here?" came a familiar voice that interrupted Grandfather. It was Roe.

"Alex, the Council of Chevrons sends greetings and a word for you—for you alone."

"I understand," said the old man. "Answer me this: how did you know?"

"How did I know where the key was?" Roe intruded. "I was here when you planted the gold in the cedar chest, of course."

"Of course," Grandfather said as he left the room.

"Alex, the council advises you to set aside ten pieces of gold. Also, always hold on to the one Princess Dora gave you personally. That one was a gift from the heart and meant for you. The remaining ten you may spend as you wish. Now, Alex, this is only advice from the council. What say you to them?" Roe said.

"Tell them I have received and accepted their advice, and as they say so, it will be. Roe, there is one problem," said Alex.

"What might that be?" asked Roe.

"I don't know which one came from the princess," said Alex.

"I see. Here, Alex." Roe gave Alex the key to the old cedar chest and pointed to the hidden keyhole. "Now, lift here and here," pointed out Roe. Alex lifted where he was told, and the bottom came out. "It's in that wool sock there, Alex." Alex took out the sock and then emptied its contents onto the bed. "Now, Alex, take one coin at a time, and drop it to the floor." Alex followed Roe's instructions.

"When the coins have all dropped to the floor, how will this tell me which one came from Princess Dora?"

"See the one that has landed on its edge; that would

be the one from her. If you doubt me, you can mark it and drop them all again, and each time will reap the same results," Roe stated.

"Thank you, Roe. That won't be necessary." Alex grinned. Alex put the one coin in his handkerchief and then placed that in his pocket. He separated the remaining coins into two stacks of ten. "The ten to be kept—where do I keep them?"

"Listen, Alex, I don't know, and no one other than you should know either. Anything else?" Roe asked.

"Yes. Send my best regards to Anton and my love to Princess Dora," Alex responded.

"As you say, Alex. As you say," Roe repeated. "Well, you do know what to do next, don't you, Alex?" Roe questioned.

"Yes, well, sure," Alex stated. Alex turned around one time, and Roe was gone.

Alex went to the front porch, where Michael and Grandfather were waiting. "I told your father you needed time alone with your reward, Alex," Grandfather said.

"What do you think, Alex?" asked Michael.

"Father, there is a give-and-take process on my mind. Please let me explain as best as I can. One thing I would ask is that you and Grandfather not ask me how I came to my decision," Alex said.

"Now, listen, Alex; you are fifteen years old—plenty old enough for most matters. It will depend on your choices whether or not I question them," Michael said sternly.

Alex looked at Grandfather as if he wanted the old man to defend him. Grandfather just waited for Alex to speak. Alex was a bit afraid to begin. Begin he did in a firm and calm manner. "The one deplume found in my hand I wish to keep, not to spend but to keep for myself."

Michael said, "Fine, go on."

"Ten pieces are to be put away by me. We may agree on how the other ten are used," Alex finished.

"Alex, why hide ten pieces?" Michael asked.

"Please, Father, are ten deplumes not enough to answer all our needs and prayers?" Alex asked.

"Well, yes, Alex, of course, much more than enough. Alex, don't answer my question with a question," Michael said.

"Sorry, Papa," said Alex.

"I don't understand the ten you want to hide, but they are yours, and you may do as you wish," Michael added.

"Two to you and Mother, two to Susan and Brad, one

for Sharrie Lee, one for Grandfather, one for Thomas and his college and whatever life he chooses, one for myself, and two to be sold and the money put into a general fund for the people of our village in need," Alex concluded.

"Alex, you have given this a lot of thought. What do you think, Father?" Michael asked.

"I think the lad is very wise as well as very generous. Why, one deplume is more than one person could need in a lifetime," said Grandfather.

"True," said Michael, "the person with the right heart and mind could do a lot of good. Alex, you're quite a good and thoughtful lad. The people of this area will be so grateful for your generosity."

"No, Father, they won't. The fund is to be set up in Grandfather's and your names. I'm proud to be a McNaire. Besides, I'm a lad, and I'd like to grow up as such. Gratitude is a wonderful thing, but it is my wish it be declared a McNaire fund, not an Alex fund," Alex finished.

"Fine, it will be as you say, Alex. Oh, one more thing, son," said Michael. "Today's Thursday. Have your mother write a note for your school. The note should say that you will not be in school tomorrow, Monday, or Tuesday due to family business. Also, tell your mother, brother, and sisters to prepare for a weekend in Yorkshire and pack for at least three days. Now, be off, so your grandfather and I can make plans," Michael said.

"All right!" Alex yelled.

"What do you think, Father?" asked Michael.

"I believe the boy has a big heart and wisdom beyond his years," Grandfather McNaire said.

When the two men went back to Grandfather's room, the key was back where they had put it. After checking the chest, they found only ten deplumes in the wool sock. "The boy's mind is set, Michael, and I don't think it a good idea to question him on where the other ten deplumes might be," Grandfather said.

"Yes, Father," Michael agreed, "but I can't help but wonder why he's split his reward as he has."

"I'm sure Alex has his reasons, and we may never understand them. However, it is up to him, and I think it best to leave it as such," Grandfather responded.

"Agreed. I guess it best to prepare for Yorkshire," Michael said.

Alex left for school the next morning with his note to excuse him from class. The rest of the McNaires planned for their weekend in Yorkshire. Michael left early that Friday to make it to the essayer's office in the big city before it closed. The Squire accompanied him as far as the city limits. They rode fast and hard, not even stopping for lunch. The family was to meet Michael at the Yorkshire Hotel Saturday afternoon. The girls were all packed, and Grandfather and Thomas had their things ready.

When Alex returned home from school, he ate a quick dinner and packed his things. When Alex was in his room, Roe showed up unannounced, as was his way.

"Alex," began Roe, "you have made some very good choices with your reward. Where are the ten pieces of gold I asked you to set aside?"

"You mean you don't know?" asked Alex.

"No, or I would not ask," Roe remarked.

"The gold is in me work boots in the closet," said Alex.

"Very well, then," Roe said. "You'll have to do better than that, for it may be a good long while before you use it."

"Okay then, Roe. Where would you have me put it?" Alex asked.

"Meet me behind the barn, Alex, and bring your reward with you," Roe said.

Alex grabbed his gold from his boot and headed for the barn through the front door. Everyone was busy, so he left unnoticed. Alex met Roe behind the barn. "Now what?" asked Alex.

"See that raspberry bush by the fence?" asked Roe.

"Yes," said Alex.

"Dig down close to the bush's roots. Dig deep." Alex did as he was told. "Now, pile stones around the entire base of the bush," said Roe.

"Okay," Alex said.

"That'll do fine—much harder to find should someone come looking while the whole family is away," said Roe. "Alex, you have a great time in Yorkshire, and I will see you when you return."

"Is the gold safe, Roe?" asked Alex.

"Yes, Alex, I'll keep an eye on it until you get back. Then you'll have to put it in a safe place that only you know about. For now, it will be fine. However, not even I should know where it is. The Council of Chevrons has plans I am not aware of and I choose not to know about. I'm sure they will be testing you from time to time. For what purpose is not for me to know."

Alex looked at the new hiding place for only a moment. When he again looked to address Roe, the wee man had vanished into thin air. Alex then returned to the house. Even Alex did not know why he hid the ten pieces of gold, but he had learned not to question the Council of Chevrons.

The next morning, the McNaire family stirred early. They packed the buckboard and headed to Yorkshire by 6 bells the girls feel asleep while Alex just enjoyed the cool breeze. Thomas nodded in and out and talked very little. In the front seat, Jean and Grandfather talked back and forth. They traveled until they came to the large shade tree by the stream. Here, they stopped for a small brunch and to stretch their legs. They were soon on the road, and they entered Yorkshire close to thirteen bells' toll.

They met up with Michael, who gave everyone their room keys. He had Thomas and Alex unload the luggage and carry it to the rooms.

"Grandfather, join me in the pub, please," Michael directed.

"Sure, son," said Grandfather.

"Father, you could not imagine the amount of money I've handled since yesterday," Michael said.

"I can imagine, Michael," Grandfather stated.

"Here is a very small portion of yours, Father." Michael handed the old man a roll of bills and a heavy change bag. "This is just for you and your short visit to Yorkshire."

"Come now, Michael, whatever will I do with so

much? This is more money than I have ever held at one time," Grandfather said.

"Spend it as you wish, Father. There is twenty times that amount in your bank account. I've kept similar amounts out for everyone—smaller ones for the children and some for Jean and me. Since each coin was of a different value, I just totaled the whole amount and broke it down as Alex asked," Michael added.

"You know, Michael, this is a once-in-a-lifetime event, not in everyone's lifetime at that. When we return home, we'll have to make some well-thought-out plans for the use of it," Grandfather said.

"Yes, Father, I agree. I've known that all along. We are McNaires and must conduct ourselves as such. By the way, Father, Squire O'Conner and two other men of his choosing will be here tomorrow. I asked him when we parted to escort us and the town's money back to the village," said Michael.

"Wise on your part," Grandfather interjected.

"I believe it best to leave most of the total here in Yorkshire until we've better planned for it," Michael finished.

"Good, son. Now let's find the rest of the clan," ended Grandfather McNaire.

Once the whole family was gathered in the lobby and Michael handed out the allotted spending money, Jean and the girls went shopping. Thomas and Alex, too, went off to see the town. Grandfather and Michael retired to the pub. It was late in the evening when everyone returned to the hotel.

"Jean," said Michael, "we may need a second wagon just to carry all you girls bought today."

"Oh, Michael, you may be right. There is still tomorrow," Jean said.

"Help me, Saint Peter." Michael smiled.

The family met in the café for lunch.

"I want you all to enjoy yourselves," Michael said. "Just because you have enough money to buy anything you want doesn't necessarily mean you need to buy everything you see. Remember this good fortune is to be used wisely. I will not have a single McNaire thinking him- or herself better than any other of our clansmen when we return home. So don't just think about yourselves; perhaps a few gifts for your friends and our neighbors would be nice." The family had dinner and retired early. Next morning they ate breakfast and broke up for their final day in Yorkshire.

"Grandfather, may I take council with you for a short while, please?" asked Michael.

"Of course you may, son," Grandfather answered.

"Father, what do you believe best for the banking of the funds?"

"Well, Michael, as you have said, leave the majority in the Yorkshire Bank. I would suppose it best to leave a portion of Alex's and Sharrie's in a trust fund, seeing as they will be in school and have a while before they know what their life goals are. If it were I, I'd leave a portion of Susan's and Thomas's in a trust but take the bulk of theirs back to the village bank. That would make it easier on them in their life choices. Mine, I'd have you transfer all of it back to the village. As for yours and Jean's, that would be entirely up to you, son," Grandfather stated.

"I see. Very well, then. You and the rest will leave tomorrow. Squire O'Conner, his two friends, and I will follow later in the day when I've finished at the bank," Michael concluded.

When Michael and Grandfather finished their planning, Squire O'Conner stepped up and bid them both hello. "Hello, Michael and Mr. McNaire. Ya both know Les Johnson and Tom Perkins."

"Of course. How are you both?" Michael said.

Grandfather nodded at the two. They entered the lobby, and the desk clerk stepped up to the counter. "Give these gents each a room, and put them on me account," Michael ordered.

"Thank you, Michael," said all three men.

"I'll get your keys. Why don't you join my father in the pub? I'll meet up with you there," Michael said.

Once at the table, Squire asked Grandfather the reason for a three-man escort. "Michael asked me to meet him here with two armed men," said Squire O'Conner.

"I believe I'll leave Michael to explain it to you," Grandfather stated. Michael handed each man his key and took a seat at the table.

"What's the news, Michael?" Squire asked.

"Well, Squire, as I'm sure Mr. McTavish has spread all over the village by now, I've found something on my farm."

"What have you found on your place, McNaire?" Squire asked.

"Gold," said Michael.

"Gold," repeated the squire. "There is no gold in our ground in these parts—at least not that I have ever heard tell of."

"True," Michael said. "Not in the ground, but a king's ransom in coined deplumes I've found."

"Ya don't say, Michael," Squire choked.

"I do say," said Michael. "They're already sold, and the earnings are in the bank. That's why I've asked you to come: to guard us on the way home."

"Smart thing to do, Michael," Squire added.

"Have ya all had any lunch?" Grandfather asked.

"No, not yet," said Mr. Johnson.

"They have a fine selection. Eat whatever you wish. It's on the McNaires."

"That won't be necessary," Squire said.

"Oh, but yes, it's a small price for what you are here to do for us," Grandfather jumped in.

"We'd do it for nothing. You know that," added Tom Perkins.

"Your services are worth a room and a few meals. Let me do as I'm able, please," Michael said.

"Fine. As you wish," Shane O'Conner said.

The day passed as the men ate, then played cards and dice as everyone began to show up for dinner. Jean went on about the gifts she bought for almost every woman in their small town. The girls gave an account of their day; then Alex and Thomas did the same. Michael just sighed and was thankful they were headed home the next day. After dinner, the children excused themselves to their rooms. The adults visited a short while before retiring for the evening.

CHAPTER 10
A NEW TOWN

Early the next morning, Michael had the buckboard pulled up to the front of the hotel. After breakfast, the children loaded it full, leaving barely enough room for passengers.

"Perkins, you ride with the wagon. Les and I will come back with Michael," the squire shouted.

Finally, the family headed back to the village. Michael, the squire, and Les headed for the bank. It took Michael more than an hour to set up the trust funds and draw out the money to take home. Finally, the three men mounted their horses.

"Home," Michael said. "Let's get there safe."

"That we will," said the squire as the men left Yorkshire

in their dust. In fact, they rode hard enough to catch up with the buckboard just before they reached the village.

The streets of the village were crowded. Really, that wasn't much of a surprise. Mr. McTavish had spread the word about the McNaires' good fortune. The buckboard pulled up at the mercantile. The three mounted horses pulled up in front of the bank. Straight inside they went, each man carrying four bags stuffed full.

Jean and the girls handed out their gifts as if it were Christmas. Thomas and Alex were almost as bad. Grandfather just sat in the buckboard shaking his head. Then there came a shout from the bank for the crowd to gather in front. After all the people had settled down in front of the bank, the mayor was summoned to come forward.

The bank president Mr. Donnely announced.

"Mayor, it is with great pleasure I give you Michael of the McNaire clan." Michael approached the mayor, shook his hand, and said, "It is with joy I present to this community of my friends, neighbors, and fellow clansmen twenty-two million Irish pounds. It is for a fund to rebuild our village into a small town. It is also for future need, as your town council seems fit to distribute it among any who have a need for it."

After several minutes of shouts and cheers, the mayor held his hand up, and the crowd became silent. "Michael McNaire, son, through what means can you afford such a gift?" the mayor asked.

"If you must know, it is by my youngest son Alex's discovery of a lost treasure he and he alone found. It was his wish that this fund be given to you all, on behalf of the McNarie Clan" Michael said.

"Thank you, Mr. McNaire. As mayor, I see a new and bright future for our village. It seems only fitting to give our soon-to-be new town a new name. Do I have the approval of the people in giving us the name befitting the donor of this most gracious gift? From this day forth, we shall be known as the folk of Alexandrea," the mayor said.

"Yes! Yes! Yes!" came from the crowd.

"So as to prevent a stampede, there will be a list posted alphabetically on the town's bulletin board. Each day, a new list will be posted until every family or person has been interviewed. After the immediate needs are met, we will hold a town council. At the council, we will discuss small business loans and a new school. Of course, I'm just the mayor. As usual, the clans will decide the future of this community. Tomorrow, with the rising of a new sun, there will come a new beginning. Until then, McNaires, we thank you. It is by my order that the McNaire family not be hounded nor bothered but left in peace. That is my final word," the mayor stated.

The McNaires enjoyed an evening meal at the White Horse Inn. While there, they visited with their friends and neighbors. Then they took the scenic route back to their farm.

***

Many changes took place during the winter months. The McNaires themselves changed very little, but their lives changed a great deal. Thomas took entrance exams and was accepted into the university in Dublin, Michael and Jean met with builders and planned to have a new house built on the soon-to-be main street of town. They left the farm to Susan and Brad as a wedding gift. Grandfather bought a small parcel of land from the owner of the White Horse Inn and had a cottage built—something comfortably sized for one person. Though the farm was left to Brad and Susan, the east field, about four acres, would be given to Alex upon his graduation from high school.

Winter, though cold and rugged, posed little threat to the McNaire clan. The season passed quickly as Alex completed his next-to-last year of school. The village had already begun to go through changes. There were new stores, and even the doctor took an office outside his home. A new hospital was in the future, and two English doctors were to move to the new city. A new elementary school was blueprinted, and a new town square was designed. There was talk of new industry moving in that would supply new jobs for generations to come. Indeed, Alexandrea would surely be put on the map.

Alex only saw Roe twice all winter. The leprechaun said it was horrible getting around in the snow—very difficult to go undetected. When he did visit, news of the war got worse; he said the princess was growing tired and becoming not at all like herself. The business of battle kept Leappy occupied, and he was still forbidden aboveground. So Alex just sent messages through Roe.

Soon, it was spring in Ireland. The construction started. Susan's wedding was the biggest event of the year, even bigger than the Founders Day event. The couple left for their honeymoon. They took two weeks to cruise through the British Isles. Grandfather was present during the building of his cottage. In fact, he even lived in it before it was completed. The McNaires' house took some time to finish because Jean kept changing her mind on some of the designs.

Alex kept to himself a lot that summer. He spent hours by the old stream pondering Anton. The family had settled down in their new quarters just before Founders Day. Alex missed working in the fields and wasn't sure where he wanted to go after he graduated come next year. He was happy to be with his family, who hadn't noticed the changes in him due to all the commotion going on in their new lifestyles. Sharrie Lee was getting ready to start her first year in grade school, Jean was running for town council, and Michael was starting a lumber mill. It was Grandfather who paid the most attention to Alex. They talked of many things but always ended up talking about Alex's time in the underground world of the leprechauns.

CHAPTER 11
VACATION FOR ALEX

It was not until the first part of the next year that Roe paid Alex a visit. Spring and summer came and went without a word from Anton. Alex was at Grandfather McNaire's cottage waiting for Grandfather to get home. He was making snowballs and throwing them at a knot in a large tree that grew in Grandfather's backyard. Alex heard the now-familiar wee voice of Roe. Alex became excited.

"Where are you, Roe?" shouted Alex.

"Over here," came the voice.

Alex followed the voice over to a small row of hedges. "Over where?" asked Alex.

Roe shook the small branches of the bush he was under. Roe let out a yelp as Alex saw the snow from the

90

branches fall. "How do your folk live in this white stuff?" complained Roe.

"I guess we just grow up with it," Alex remarked. "How be you, Roe?"

"Cold at the moment, but other than that, I'm faring quite well, thank you. You, Alex, how be yourself?" Roe asked.

"Don't know for sure," responded Alex. "This *being rich* thing is getting dull. I mean, I really appreciate all that it has done for my family and our town. It's just I miss the closeness of the way things used to be. Do you understand?"

"I believe I can, Alex. I have some news that may interest you," said Roe.

"Yes, and what might that be, Roe?"

"Quantine," said Roe.

"Haven't heard that word in a long time. It's extinct now, isn't it?" asked Alex.

"We thought that to be true. Our troops have moved Coret and Trogg far enough south to uncover new sprouts shooting up all over the barren wasteland close to Twin Sisters Falls." (*map*)

"Wonderful news! A lot of good that does me now," said Alex.

"Could be," added Roe.

"Whatever do you mean, Roe?" Alex asked.

"Just that if you ever want to visit Anton, it will soon be possible," Roe remarked.

"What? I never dreamed—that is, I would love to see my friends, but I never thought it possible. When?" Alex asked.

"Alex, quantine is a very hearty wild plant that takes a few months to grow. It first must develop buds. The milk of the plant is most effective for our use just before the bud blossoms. After it flowers, the milk is too weak to be of any use," Roe explained. "Then again, Alex, the war is still not won. Perhaps at a later time would be better."

"I do have school, but I have three months off starting in the spring. That's a few months from now," said Alex.

"You're a true lover of my people, Alex," said Roe. "It could be dangerous. Or suppose for some reason you couldn't make it back in time?"

"True," said Alex. "Let's make plans just the same. Then we will see if there comes a time to put a plan to use."

"Very well, Alex. I'll take care of my part, sure enough. You'll have to tend to your daily affairs above ground. I'll see you again before the plant buds," Roe said.

"Thank you, Roe. Send my best wishes to the king, princess, and dear friends, please." Alex smiled.

"As you wish, They send you their love and respect as well" said Roe.

As Alex departed, turning in a circle, he ran straight into Grandfather. "Ah, Alex, my lad, what you doing outside? Come in, and have some hot cocoa," Grandfather said.

Once inside, Alex could barely slow down enough for Grandfather McNaire to understand him. Alex had to be careful in his choice of words. He managed not to mention quantine but was able to convince the old man of the possibility of returning to Anton.

"Alex, are you sure? I mean, you don't even know how you got there the first time. Even more important, you don't know how you got back," said Grandfather.

"That's all true. The leprechauns know, and that's good enough for me," Alex explained.

"Seems you put a lot of trust into these little creatures," proclaimed Grandfather.

"If they had wished me harm, Grandfather, they would never have sent me back—certainly not have rewarded me so generously," responded Alex.

"I see your point, son. Still, it sounds risky to me," Grandfather stated.

"I am sorry you feel that way, Grandfather. I will need your help just the same," said Alex.

"In what manner can I help, Alex?" asked Grandfather.

"Well, spring break is a few months off. I'm sure if I asked for a vacation to just about anywhere, I wouldn't be allowed to go alone even though I'm sixteen. If you'd be willing to vouch for me by saying you'd accompany me, I'm sure to be granted my request," Alex said.

"I see. What is it that I'm to do while you are gone?" questioned Grandfather.

"Isn't there any site in the world you'd like to see? Simply take the time to enjoy your dreams," said Alex.

"I've always wanted to visit England. The palaces, the place where all the artwork is. Oh, where is that?"

"Paris, France, Grandfather. It's called the Louvre." Grandfather went on and on until Alex interrupted. "By the way, Grandfather, could you do all that in three weeks?"

"Yes, yes, I could, Alex," said Grandfather McNaire.

"Then can we strike a deal?" asked Alex.

"What kind of a deal? I could take the trip on me

own, without covering you with a wee tale to your folks," said Grandfather.

"Of course you could. I guess I'll have to come up with something different to do. I just thought I'd ask," Alex said.

"Alex, think a minute here. What if something were to happen? Say, for whatever reason, you didn't make it back. Whatever could I tell your parents?" Grandfather stated.

"Yes, of course it is too much to ask," said Alex. "I'll be running along now. See you tomorrow."

"Hold up, Alex. I'll think on it a spell. If you come up with something different, you would let me know first, wouldn't you?" Grandfather asked.

"Sure, I mean, yes, of course, sir," Alex said as he left the cottage.

Grandfather kicked off his boots and put a log on the fire. He sat back in his easy chair and drifted off to sleep. Sometime in the middle of the night, the old man was awakened by a pulling on his sock. He shook his leg and settled back. Nearly asleep, he felt the tug again. "What is it?" he asked as he bent over to take a look.

"Now listen here, you grumpy old giant. If you throw

me across the room again, I'll make sure your socks catch aflame."

"Oh, it's you, Roe," said Grandfather.

"Yes, it is, and I've come to parley with you about Alex."

"Oh, you overheard our conversation?"

"Yes, I did. It is my job to look over Alex. I'll have you know, Mr. McNaire, Alex is safe with my people. We would do our best to see him to and from Anton. You have my word on that. Contrary to what you may have heard about us, we keep our word, or else we don't give it," said Roe.

"I see," Grandfather said. "I intended to tell Alex yes anyway, Roe. Your reassurance of his safety still comforts me just the same."

"It is unusual for me to say this, sir, but thank you. It will mean a lot to Alex's friends, who miss him more each day. Besides, to hear Alex say it. It would do him a world of good," stated Roe. "I think so too," said Grandfather.

Roe asked the old man to close his eyes and count to five. This Grandfather did, and when he opened his eyes again, Roe was gone. *Quick little folks, aren't they?* thought Grandfather. He smacked his lips a few times and then drifted back off to sleep.

The next day was Sunday, a day the family spent together. Of course, Thomas was away at the university, but all the rest showed up at Brad and Susan's newly decorated farmhouse.

"Good to see you all," said Susan. Michael, Jean, Sharrie Lee, and Alex had picked up Grandfather at his cottage, so they all arrived together. "Come in. Come in out of the cold," said Susan. Brad was stocking the fireplace in the living room when Michael, Alex, and Grandfather walked in.

"Hello, son," said Michael.

"Hello, sir, and hello to you all," said Brad. "I'll fetch some drinks and be right back."

"They've sure fixed up the place, haven't they?" Michael stated.

"Yes, they have," Grandfather agreed.

"It still feels like home to me," Alex commented.

"Yes, it does in a way," said Grandfather.

The girls were finishing setting the table while the men chatted of the past week's news. Dinner was called, and they all sat down to a wonderfully prepared feast.

"Your mother has taught you well, Susan," said Michael.

"Now, Michael, I've only taught her the basics. Most of these dishes are her own creations," Jean responded.

"Thank you, Mother," said Susan.

As they ate, the conversation was lighthearted and at times humorous. As dinner drew to a close, Grandfather tapped his spoon on his glass. Everyone was quiet as he said, "I have an announcement to make. In all my years, I've wanted to visit the remote castles and the hillsides of England and to explore the fine arts of Paris in France. So this spring, I shall do so."

"Wonderful," said Jean.

"Well deserved too," said Michael.

"With your permission, I've planned my little adventure around Alex's spring break. I've done so in hopes he might accompany me."

"Oh yes, Grandfather, if I may. Father, could I?" asked Alex.

"I see no reason why you couldn't. I'll leave it up to your mother," said Michael.

"Of course, Alex. It would not only be fun but a great learning experience for you," finished Jean. Small conversations broke out as dinner ended.

"Thank you, Grandfather. Thank you so very much," Alex said.

"My pleasure, lad," said Grandfather McNaire.

After dinner, the men gathered in the living room, soon to be joined by the female McNaires.

"That's wonderful news, Mr. McNaire. I hope this doesn't dampen your moment, but Susan has a bit of good news to share with you all. Susan," said Brad.

"Mother and Father, you are soon to be grandparents, and Grandfather, you'll be a great-grandfather, literally."

"That's wonderful news, Susan."

"How far along are you?" asked Jean.

"About three months," said Susan.

"*Uncle Alex.* I like the sound of that," said Alex.

"Yes, it has been a great day in the McNaire house," said Jean.

"It's still getting darker out sooner these days. We would best be heading home," said Michael. As they said their good-byes at the door, Susan got a hug from everyone, including Alex.

CHAPTER 12
RETURN TO ANTON

Alex could hardly wait to tell Roe to send a message of his return. That winter was cold and bitter. It seemed to drag on and on. It was mid-March before the frigid weather broke. *It is about time to put away the long johns and heavy winter coats,* he thought.

Alex didn't visit his nap tree for months, until one Saturday the sun shined enough to warm the air and melt the snow. Alex took a walk from town to his favorite spot near the newly cut-up tree. All that was left was a chopped-up stump on which he sat. He kept hoping Roe would show up, but the day passed without a sign. Spring break was just a few weeks off. Alex thought, *I hope all is well in Anton and Roe has carried through on his end.*

It came to be Sunday afternoon. Alex had just left

Grandfather's cottage. They decided to take a stagecoach to Dublin to start Grandfather's vacation. The first stop would be Antwerp, a small village a few hours away from Alexandrea. Alex would part company with Grandfather and double back to meet Roe. He just didn't know where or when.

A whistle from a cove of trees brought Alex's attention back to where he was. Then he heard it again—faint, yet he knew it was there. He walked to the cove, in the midst of which sat Roe. Roe was just sitting, puffing on his long-stemmed pipe.

"Surprise! Hey, Alex," said Roe.

"Where you been, Roe?" Alex asked.

"Now, Alex, it's not polite to ask such a thing of a leprechaun," Roe answered. "Besides, you wouldn't understand half of what I told you."

"I suppose. What about the quantine? Is it ready?" questioned Alex.

"Yes, it is ready. Are you?" asked Roe.

"Yes, all but the final details," Alex answered.

"Okay, Alex, what's your plan?" Alex filled Roe in on what he and Grandfather McNaire had come up with. "Fine so far, Alex. You know, it'll take about three days before you're small enough to travel with me," Roe stated.

"Where am I to hide for three days?" asked Alex.

"What about the cottage? Your grandfather will be gone," said Roe.

"Yes, but I need to walk a distance from Antwerp. However, if the timing is right, I can sneak in after dark," said Alex.

"That's the plan then," Roe said. "I'll meet you in the cottage two weeks from Tuesday."

"Fine, that will be the time then," Alex said. The two exchanged farewells and words to send to Anton and then parted company.

It started to warm up around the Emerald Isle by the time two more weeks had passed. Alex packed his luggage for the supposed trip with Grandfather. He carried it to the cottage, where the two were to load it onto the stagecoach in front of the White Horse Inn. Alex realized he had overlooked something: the luggage. Surely, he didn't want to hike from Antwerp with luggage. Grandfather told him not to worry; they would have the stage stop keeper put it in storage until their return.

Finally, the day came for their departure. The family and some friends showed up to see the stagecoach off. As the whip snapped and the horse bolted, Alex jerked back as he waved good-bye. Soon, all that could be seen was a cloud of dust rising from the road. It was a short trip to Antwerp, but it would seem twice as long walking back, if not more.

The stage pulled into the Antwerp mercantile. The driver took off the mailbag as Alex unloaded his own luggage. The stage line clerk checked Alex's luggage into a storage bin and gave him a receipt. The driver announced, "All aboard." Then he looked at Alex and said, "Stage is leaving, lad. You have a round-trip ticket, don't you?"

"Yes, sir, I do," Alex commented. Alex went to the stage door and gave his ticket and storage receipt to Grandfather. "Since I don't think I can keep track of them where I am going, hold these, and I'll meet you right here in two weeks' time," Alex said.

"Alex, if you're more than a day late, it could be the life of me," Grandfather said.

"I'll be fine. You'll see," Alex stated. He stepped back from the coach and waved the driver off. The stage pulled out, and Alex took the long road back to Grandfather's cottage. He had to stop twice to rest. The fact was it helped kill time. He wanted it to be nightfall when he reached Alexandrea.

It had been dark for more than an hour when Alex sneaked behind the White Horse Inn. When he entered the cottage, it was pitch-black. "Roe? Are you here?" whispered Alex.

"Yes, Alex. Cover the windows, lad. A candle's light would alert the townsfolk someone is here." Alex fumbled for Grandfather's bed and pulled the cover off. Then he placed it over the two windows facing the White Horse. "Alex, there is enough quantine here to get you to the size we need. The only drawback is you're going to sleep a lot over the next three days," said Roe.

"Oh," gasped Alex. "Clothes. What about clothes?" Alex asked.

"I've brought your clothes from Sir Satchen's. You'll have to make do with whatever keeps you covered until they fit is all," Roe replied.

"Let's start," said Alex.

"Very well," said Roe. "I'll nurse you till you're the proper size. Here, take this and then this honey-covered cracker. The honey cuts the bite of the quantine. The milk is very bitter—more bitter than the first time you tasted it. That was old, and this is fresh."

Alex did as he was directed. It didn't take more than a few minutes before Alex became drowsy and fell asleep. It was well into the second day of taking doses every six to eight hours that a change in Alex's size took place. He mostly noticed it in his socks and shoes. By midmorning of the third day, Alex was swimming in his clothes, so he started wrapping himself in bath towels. The shrinking quickened after that. As the sun rose on the fourth day, Alex dressed in his leprechaun attire and was ready for his adventurous visit.

CHAPTER 13
DANGEROUS WATERS

Alex had spent three days and four nights of his vacation in Grandfather McNaire's cottage. He was becoming more and more anxious to start his visit, so Roe had to slow him down a bit.

"Alex, I know you want to hurry, but you must listen to me first. Once we are underground, things will become instantly dangerous. Though above ground we are a few miles from Clarion, when we descend, we will be taken almost to the front gates of the city. Though Trogg and Coret have been pushed back, some of their ugly troops and foul creatures still lurk in the shadows. They are spies, and they take no prisoners."

"Thank you, Roe, but when we get close, I'll know if

they are around. I haven't forgotten that terrible smell of theirs," said Alex.

"I see," said Roe.

The two walked a short distance from Grandfather's back door. Under a large mulberry bush, where a large outcrop of rocks stood, they slithered their way among them. They found an entryway of six steps to a pathway that gradually led downward. It was a little dark. Roe lit a torch as they proceeded.

It seemed it would go on forever. Down and down they walked. At first, the ground had cut-off roots along the walls. Soon, the walls turned to ground studded with small rocks. Eventually, the small tunnel opened wider into smoothly shaved walls of stone. It became wide enough that Alex could detect faint blue light from the Tower of Clarion. Once they entered the cavernous space of the kingdom, Alex recalled his first experience in Clarion. He saw the huge pile of boulders. Like a mountain, it ran up and packed in among the roots of Alex's favorite tree—at least what was left of it. The mountain of stone hid Clarion from humans, should they dig up the stump, which was not likely. They'd leave the stump to rot and eventually become level with the ground, plowed over or left to grass.

"Now, Alex, keep your eyes and ears open—in your case, your nose as well. We will make our way to Anton by way of the river. I have a small flat-bottomed boat around a bend just upstream," said Roe.

As the two took to the far bank along the wall, Alex recalled the hundreds of pairs of feet he had seen with wheelbarrows. They had carried stones to hide Clarion. He felt strange now walking the same path as they had. *The river,* he thought, *will take us to Anton, as it did on my first adventure.*

By the time the two of them reached the small boat, it was dark blue in the underground kingdom, indicating that soon it would be nightfall. Roe and Alex decided to make up a camp for the night. Now that Alex was the proper size, he only needed quantine every twelve hours; as they were settling in, he needed a dose. They curled up in sleeping bags that had been left in the boat. Alex dreamed of the fields of Aurelie from Princess Dora's songs. He slept soundly through the night.

When he awoke, the cavern contained a pinkish haze. Alex and Roe ate honey and wafers, loaded the small boat, and headed upriver. Their next stop was the Falls of Aphilia. (**map**) As Alex took his turn with the dredging pole, he noticed strange things floating in the water.

There were pieces of wood, arrows, clothing, and scraps of leather. *From the war,* he thought.

Roe shouted to Alex to stop the small craft. "What's this all about?" shouted Alex back.

"We are not alone here, Alex. There is something in the water," said Roe.

"Yes, I see all the stuff floating around," said Alex.

"No, under the water," snapped Roe. "Make for shore. Quick, Alex, quick."

They both dredged as hard and as fast as they could. Alex glanced behind him. He saw what looked to be a rock, only this rock was moving and closing in on them. Just in time, they pulled the boat to shore and dragged it inland. A giant turtle lifted its head out of the water, its neck fully extended. Its huge mouth snapped closed, making a sound like two trees falling on top of each other. Alex recalled Yota's description of such turtles: "They can sink a barge." Alex felt a great relief pass over him.

They had just made it through an up-close and real life-and-death experience. Roe told Alex it was best to portage the boat for the rest of the day. "We are still too close to Clarion. Not all of Trogg's creatures retreated with him. Be alert; there are also some very large serpents about."

"Snakes!" yelled Alex.

"Yes, and they have been known to attack on land as well as in the water," answered Roe.

The two carried the boat and supplies over land. They stopped every hour or so for rest and refreshment. Alex stayed constantly on the lookout for snakes. He would rather take his chances with the turtles. It was late in the day when they first heard the roar from the Falls of Aphilia. Alex remembered that sound also.

"We are not going to make the falls before it becomes too dark to travel," said Roe.

"What about taking a torch and going back to the river?" asked Alex.

"No way," said Roe. "The enemy loves the night and could spot a floating torch from kilometers away."

"Very well, then, we will put up for one more night," replied Alex.

"We will be in Anton tomorrow, barring any further troubles. Once at the falls, we can relaunch the boat and make much quicker time," said Roe. "Trogglites are not this far upriver. At least none have been reported. The snakes and turtles hate the falls because of her swift currents. We should be safe from here on. Your quantine?" asked Roe.

"Yes, of course," said Alex. He knew he was getting

used to the milk because the drowsy effect was growing weaker and weaker. Roe and Alex talked into the night about Alex's last visit. Roe seemed surprised to hear of Alex and the band of Royal Children.

Sometime during the night, Alex drifted off to sleep. The roar of the falls had become so familiar that Alex could not hear Roe calling his name. So Roe tugged on his ear once or twice. "Hey now," snapped Alex, "you scared me to death. I thought at first a snake was sucking on me ear—you know, to see how I tasted."

"No, Alex, it's just me, and you're welcome," said Roe.

"Welcome for what?" asked Alex.

"You do wish to see Anton today, don't you?" asked Roe.

"Yes. Thank you, Roe, of course I do," answered Alex.

After a quick wafer and honey, they rolled up the sleeping gear, pushed the boat into the water, threw in the gear, and headed off almost in a mechanical motion. The poles were hard to push at first because of the backflow of water from the falls. Once they cleared the falls' current, they moved along smoothly and at a quicker speed.

Alex felt refreshed and relieved. *The troubled waters are behind us now. We will be in Anton soon. I will see Dora again, after what has seemed like a lifetime,* Alex thought.

CHAPTER 14
REUNITED

When they drew close enough to Anton, Alex could hear a calliope playing. Then the city came into view, and Alex let out a sigh.

"Excited?" questioned Roe.

"Yes, yes, of course," said Alex.

The boat pulled into the dock, and Alex recognized the royal craft tied off there. His mind flashed back to memories he had of the condole, such as the last time he had ridden in it. There was only one guard at the dock. The battlefields were far to the south.

The guard greeted them by name. "You are to proceed at once to the council chambers. We knew you were coming, but a precise time was never determined."

"Thank you," answered Roe.

Alex and Roe walked up the pathway past the fountains in the small park to the council hall. Two guards stood at the massive doors to the Council of Chevrons. They snapped to attention and grabbed the hilts of their swords. This was a salute to Alex, though he didn't know it at the time.

Once inside, they were escorted to the king's chambers and asked to wait. This they did as Roe could see the mounting anticipation on Alex's face. "It won't be long now," said Roe.

"It has been too long already," stated Alex. Roe had become friends with Alex over the past few months. He actually knew very little about Alex's first visit, and he was not at all familiar with Alex's services to the Kingdom of Anton.

As the chamber doors opened, in walked the king with a smile on his face. "Alex, it is so good to see you, lad," said King Anton. "How fare you, me lad?" asked Anton.

"I fare well, Great King, and how may you be?" said Alex.

"Fine, considering it does my heart good to see you, Alex. I'm sure Dora and the court of Royal Children will feel the same," responded the king.

"Where is the princess?" Alex caught himself and said, "I'm sorry, sir. What I mean is when I may see her."

"In a few moments, Alex. I've sent for her. She doesn't know for what yet. So she will be surprised that at last you are here," said Anton.

"Thank you, sir," replied Alex.

The three had just sat down when a knock came at the door. "Come in," said the king. As the door opened, Alex and Roe stood up. In the door walked Princess Dora. Alex's heart jumped, and his face turned red.

"Why, Alex, you are blushing," said Princess Dora as she walked up to Alex. He fell to one knee, as did Roe. "Come, come," said Dora, "such a welcome from an old friend. Rise," instructed Dora. Then suddenly and quite surprisingly, she gave Alex a long hug.

The king's eyebrows rose as he spoke. "Dora, take it easy, and let the lad breathe."

"Alex, it is so wonderful to have you here," said Dora.

Alex caught his breath, then replied, "It is great to be back and to see you again."

"Alex, I'll send for my barber. Few saw you approach and enter Anton. We need to create a beard for you, so as to blend in with my people." said Anton.

"Yes, of course, sir," stated Alex.

"You may not be aware, but you are a hero of sorts to my people. If they should want to see you, it must be as Leappy's cousin," added Anton.

"Yes, King Anton, I do understand. That is, looking like a leprechaun is important, but the hero thing—I'm lost on that part," commented Alex.

"It took some time getting the reports back from Clarion. Your story is being told by young and old alike throughout the kingdom. It seems you led the tarantulas of Trogg to their deaths, acting as a sacrifice. Your friend and our hero, Brock, gave his life in that same battle. They found you unconscious and near death. Yota had you taken above ground before you recovered to your full size, which I was told happened very quickly. We here in the kingdom are honored to see you. The fact that you would risk yourself for my people, your friends, touches my heart deeply," said Anton.

"As well does it touch mine," stated Dora. "Your snuggery at Satchen's is as you left it when you departed for war. In fact, Satchen himself is anxious to see you. If the king can wait for a longer visit tomorrow, I will escort you to his abode myself," added the princess.

"I know my way there, though I would be honored to have your company," said Alex.

"Father, with your permission?" said Dora.

"By all means," answered King Anton. "Roe, you leave shortly afterward as to escort the princess back to the tower," ordered Anton.

"As you say," replied Roe.

Alex and Dora began their short stroll to Satchen's. "Alex, I have missed you so," said Dora.

"I, too, have missed you. Not a day has gone by when I haven't thought of you and Anton," remarked Alex.

"That's sweet," said Dora as she took Alex by the hand.

"Dora, you haven't forgotten I am a human, have you?" asked Alex.

"That does not matter. Who you are, not what you are, is what matters most. I am so happy to see you, Alex, regardless of what you may be," said Dora.

Alex blushed and was at a loss for words. *Well, Thomas,* thought Alex, *you were right.* Alex remembered his older brother telling him that there would come a time when he thought of girls in a different way than being odd and no fun.

They arrived at Sir Satchen's front gate with Roe a minute or so behind them. It was there Alex received his very first kiss—from a princess at that. His head spinning, he thought no one would ever believe this.

"Until tomorrow, Alex," voiced Dora as Roe came into sight.

"Yes, Princess," said Alex.

"Alex, you may call me Dora when we are alone." Dora smiled.

"Thank you. I shall, as you say, see you tomorrow," said Alex. Dora turned and walked to Roe. Then she turned and waved to Alex. Alex returned the wave and turned to Satchen's front door. Alex knocked, and the butler answered the door.

"Come in, Sir Alex. Councilman Satchen has been expecting you." Alex kind of puffed up his chest at being called *sir* and thanked the butler. "This way, please. Satchen waits in his den," stated the butler.

As they entered the room, Satchen rose from his desk and stuck out his hand to Alex. Alex shook his hand. "Welcome, Alex," said Satchen.

"Good to see you again, sir," said Alex.

At that moment, a knock came at the front door. It was the barber sent by King Anton. "You may show him to the study," said Satchen.

As the barber came into the room, he said hello first

to Satchen and then to Alex. Then he put his barber bag down and pulled up a straight-backed chair. "If you will sit here, Alex. I've been sent to do your beard," the barber stated.

Alex took the seat. As the barber worked, he continued the conversation with Satchen. "Leappy will be pleased to see you," said Satchen.

"When may that be?" asked Alex.

"Soon, Alex. Word has been sent of your arrival. The return message was Gordon and Leappy would be given a short leave from the war to return to Anton. As to when that might be, I expect any day now," responded Satchen.

The barber finished Alex's beard and began to clean up. Satchen asked Alex to come to the dining room for a bit of dinner. Alex and Satchen ate and talked for an hour or so. Then Satchen mentioned the late hour. "I'll see you at breakfast, Alex. You know the way to your quarters?" asked Satchen.

"Yes, I remember, sir. And thank you, sir, for everything," said Alex.

As Alex entered his room, he noticed it was just as he had left it. It was a little cleaner perhaps, but still as he recalled it. There were fresh and folded clothes on a chair. Next to the chair on a table sat a new dark green hat with a silver buckle. Alex fell fast asleep as soon as he climbed into the bed.

When Alex awoke the next morning, he felt refreshed and anxious to meet the day. He cleaned up and got dressed in his new attire. He met Satchen at the table for breakfast.

"You look more like the Alex I remember," said Satchen.

"Thank you, sir. I feel much more alive than I did yesterday," replied Alex.

"Yes, well, I'm off to council. You may take the liberty to go anywhere within Anton but not beyond its boundaries without military escort," warned Satchen.

"Yes, sir," said Alex.

Alex walked through the park to the Tower of Anton. He looked up at the tall structure to see Dora looking down at him.

"Good morning, Alex. I'll be right down. Stay where you are." Dora smiled. Alex waited at the entrance to the tower until Dora appeared. They hugged.

"Hello, Dora. Could we talk?" asked Alex.

"Of course. Let's sit in the park. It's a beautiful day," answered the princess.

"Dora, how is Jessica?" asked Alex.

"Not at all like herself ever since Brock's body was brought back. She still, until this very day, spends endless hours at his place of wait," stated Dora.

"Place of wait?" asked Alex.

"Yes—where one is put until his trip down the River of No Return," replied Dora.

"How long does one wait?" questioned Alex.

"However long it takes for everything to be ready. In the case of Brock, his companions are still at war. He will wait until his family and friends can all be present to see him off properly," said Dora.

"Have you any news of Leappy and Gordon?" inquired Alex.

"Yes, they have been sent word of your arrival. Runners were sent early yesterday. They are deep in the Southern Frontier. It will take a day or two, but they will come with haste," said Dora. "It's still hard to believe you've come back, Alex. Weren't you afraid?"

"I really didn't have a thought, except of seeing you and the band of Royal Children. I had not thought of the danger until already underground on the river to Anton. Still, I would fight for you and your kind," stated Alex.

"I'm sure you would," said Dora. "But you are only here for a visit—a short one at that. Let's not waste it with worry. Besides, the battles are far off, and at least for now, Anton is safe. Trogg and Coret have numbers on their side, while, on the other hand, we have Yota and your friends on ours. As long as Trogg retreats, we are winning."

Alex and Dora spent the entire day together and planned a picnic on the Island of Royal Children, where Alex first met her and heard the Tale of Seven Crystals. It seemed like ages ago to him.

The next day came, and Alex and Dora took her condole to the island. Roe and another guard followed and anchored offshore to watch over the princess.

"Alex, have you the gift I gave you the day you left for war?" asked Dora.

"Yes, Princess, I do," answered Alex.

"Good," said Dora.

"Still, I think the reward was too generous," said Alex.

"Alex, if you only knew how very much this kingdom feels for you. To go place yourself in danger to protect us deserves the greatest reward we can offer. If you had not taken Trogg's terrible creatures to the catapults, the war may be over now. We all may have been dead or at least at his horrible mercy. Of course, with your courage, you carry humility. That is the mark of a true hero. Let it be known, Alex, I felt that way about you before you left for war," said Dora.

"I don't understand. I did what I thought best—no more and no less," said Alex.

"Yes, you did, but no one else would have," Dora stated.

"Please, Princess, Brock gave his life for this kingdom," said Alex.

"Yes, he did, but had it not been for your courage, he would not have thought of closing the catapult range," said Dora.

"That really doesn't make me feel better about his death," responded Alex.

"It was his choice to go; you did not make him," said Dora.

"Yes, I know," replied Alex.

As the light became faintly blue, Dora and Alex boarded the royal condole to head back to the docks of Anton. They were met partway by a messenger in a small craft. "At your pardon, Princess, but Alex has been summoned by the king," declared the messenger.

Alex quickened his pace and with ease docked. Roe's vessel pulled in next to him. "Roe, please escort the princess wherever she wishes." With that statement, Alex took off at a run to the Council of Chevrons.

When Alex reached the hall, he was taken to Satchen's chambers. Satchen opened the door and asked Alex to follow him to the council hall. The doors swung open wide, and Alex gasped. The hall was decorated, and trumpets sounded. The councilmen stood as Alex entered the room. A feast had been prepared in his honor.

"Please, your place is set at the crown of the horseshoe table," said Satchen.

Alex walked his way around and took his seat. As Alex sat, the council members sat. A moment later, the trumpets sounded again. King Anton entered the room and took his seat upon the throne. Silence filled the hall as a squire handed a scroll to the king.

"Sir Alex, rise, and come forth," commanded Anton. Alex did as directed and stood before the throne. "In the name of Aurelie, I ask that you kneel. Do you, Alex, believe and accept that Anton is a kingdom worth defending unto death?"

"Yes," said Alex.

"You shall from this day forward be known as Sir Alex, knight to the king." Anton rose, drew his long sword, and tapped Alex on each shoulder. He then sheathed his sword and sat back upon his throne. "Rise, Sir Alex," said Anton.

As Alex stood, cheers filled the great chamber. The princess, in full royal dress, crown and all, approached Alex. "With the love of my people, I present you with this medal of valor for your bravery and courage in the fields of battle at grave risk to your own life," said Dora. Alex bent his head down as Dora placed a jeweled cross of gold and diamonds on a purple ribbon around his neck.

More cheers came until King Anton rose. Silence fell on the great hall. All eyes were on the king. His gaze was directed to the council chambers' doors. Slowly, everyone turned to see what he was staring at. The door stood open wide. There in full armor stood Yota, Leappy, and Gordon.

"If at all possible, the day is even greater in Anton," said the king. "Enter, Yota and companions; enter, and feast with us. Bring in a table of honor for our heroes of battle. Place it in the center, where I shall eat with my warriors."

Quickly, everyone sat. Servants brought in another long table. Cloths, dishes, candles, and glasses seemed to appear out of the air as servants set the table. As quickly as they came, the servants were gone.

Anton and Princess Dora joined Yota, Leappy, and Gordon at the newly set table. Alex had waited as long as he could. He stood and dashed toward Leappy. Before he could reach Leappy, Leappy had snapped to attention and put one hand on the hilt of his sword and the other hand to his chest in a salute to Alex.

"Come now, Leappy. What is all that?" asked Alex.

Leappy didn't answer. Alex returned the salute by putting one hand to his chest. Then Leappy replied, "You are a knight to the king and deserve much more than a salute."

Alex threw his arms around his old friend and said, "This is all I deserve." Leappy returned the hug, and cheers filled the hall again.

Alex saluted Gordon and shook his hand. "It is good to see you again, Gordon."

"The same to you, Sir Alex," said Gordon.

As Yota stood tall waiting to salute Alex, Alex put his hand up as if to say *wait*. Then he saluted Yota first—not quite the custom, but Yota, who seldom smiled, smiled and returned the salute. "With honor and great pleasure to see you again," said Yota.

"Yes, Yota, I am very much honored, and a great pleasure to see you again too." Alex motioned to Gordon to take his place at the head of the table. Then Alex sat down next to Yota.

"Alex, I am pleased that you would sit with me."

"As a friend," said Alex.

"Yes, I know, but your place is at the head of the table in the seat of honor," said Yota.

"Next to you, Yota, anywhere I sat would be a seat of honor," said Alex. Again, cheers broke out in the chamber.

"Thank you, Alex," said Yota.

"Let the feast begin," announced Anton. As the music played and the servants brought out plate after plate of food, conversations began throughout the great hall.

"I knew Leappy and Gordon were coming, but I never thought I'd be able to see you," Alex addressed Yota.

"The time was right. We have fought long and hard and believe we may push Trogg and Coret back into their swamps. I'm not sure why, but at times, it seems a little too easy," proclaimed Yota. "I might be wrong, but it is possible Trogg is pulling a maneuver on me I have not yet thought possible."

"You are a great general and a leader to be feared. Why doubt the possibility that those two evil brothers are on the verge of defeat against your forces?" asked Alex.

"It just seems to me that they would be fighting more

desperately; that's all. Enough about war, Alex. Let's make merry while we may. I came with Leappy and Gordon so our dear friend and your companion, Brock, could be sent on his final journey down the River of No Return."

"I am sorry," said Alex.

"Yes, we all are, Alex, but his and your sacrifice saved Clarion and rid us of those monsters, which could have otherwise turned this war into a victory for the black-hearted brothers," stated Yota.

"Come on now, Yota. I'm no hero; I'm just a lad," said Alex.

"Perhaps where you come from, Alex, but not here. Here, the future of my race shall remember the Battle of Clarion and you for generations—you, as one who served to his ultimate best," finished Yota. Then the two friends began to eat and laugh.

The night became more and more joyful. After the feast came a glorious ball. The guests danced until the light in the kingdom turned pinkish, which meant dawn's arrival.

Alex spent some special time with Leappy and Gordon. Mostly the conversation was on the tricks and fun of Alex's first visit to Anton. As the three warriors retired for the night, Alex walked Dora to her door. They sat on the steps to the tower.

"Late afternoon or early evening, there will be a ceremony for Brock, Alex. The blacksmiths and tailors have reworked your armor and weapons. The tailor added plumes and ropes to display your knighthood. It will all be delivered to Satchen's as you rest. It was thought you'd want to be presented as the soldier you were when your friend fell in combat," said Dora.

"Thank you, Princess," said Alex.

"It is *Dora*, Alex."

"Yes, I am sorry, Dora. It is very late. The feast and dancing have made me pretty tired," said Alex.

"I know, Alex. I hope you are awake enough to appreciate what I'm about to tell you. It has been well thought out," said Dora.

"Go on now, Dora. What is it?" asked Alex.

"I know this may sound selfish and maybe out of line to you. In my heart, I wish it were possible for you to stay. I mean, I know you have your family and friends above ground, and probably a girlfriend or two. It's just I'm so much happier when you're around. I can hardly bear you being out of sight," said Dora.

"Hold on a minute, Dora. Are you sure you're not

overtired? I can't keep my mind from thinking about you and Anton. But I can't stay. I mean, how could I?" asked Alex. "No, I don't have a girlfriend or two. My family is fine and off on their own journeys through life. I can't just disappear. I sure couldn't explain coming to live here."

"Yes, yes, yes, Alex, I know," said Dora. "It sounds like you have thought about it some."

"Yes, I have, and I just don't see how I can live in two places," said Alex.

"It's late, Alex. We will leave this subject for a better time. I only meant to say … I think it's called love."

"What!" started Alex. "Love? What, love! Now, Dora, I'm too young for love, whatever that means, and love?" questioned Alex. Then Dora kissed him. Alex became silent. Again, his head spun, and he whispered, "Hm, *love*. I guess it could be."

"Yes, it could be," stated Dora.

"Yes, good night, Dora. Dora, just a minute. Could we try the kiss thing again?"

"Happy to, Alex." Dora smiled.

Again, Alex became lightheaded and felt warm all over. "Yes, it could be; it certainly could be." He kept mumbling to himself as he turned from Dora.

CHAPTER 15
RIVER OF NO RETURN

Alex tossed and turned the remainder of the night. As soon as he felt settled with being a human lad, he thought of Dora and being a knight to the king, which would start him wondering again. Still, he rose the next morning to the sound of the butler calling his name from the door to his room.

"Good morning. Your things arrived earlier this morning. They are in your closet," said the butler.

"Thank you," answered Alex. He poured water into a basin and washed up.

When he opened the closet, he stepped back in surprise. His old armor was buffed and shining. He dressed quickly and stepped in front of the mirror. Surely, no one above ground would believe the sight he made. Alex himself was finding it difficult to believe. He strapped on his sword and dagger. They, too, had been buffed and cleaned. The edges were sharpened, and the sword's hilt had been redone. In bronze and silver was his name. It read, "Sir Alex." Along the top edge of the blade inlaid with gold lettering was the title "Knight to the King of Anton."

The dagger was capped with a serpent's head, and the blade was inscribed with elfin symbols Alex could not understand. He then admired his breastplate. A few ropes had been added over each shoulder; there was one of braided gold and one of deep purple. Alex thought it strange, being that purple was a signature color for royalty in his world. He dismissed the notion and continued to dress.

On top of the dresser was a new addition to his suit of armor: a helmet, which he tried on and found it fit perfectly. One long pure-white plume sticking out of the center top lay restfully down the back of the helmet. Alex hadn't worn a helmet in his brief military career, so he found it to be amusing and quite appealing. He stuck the helmet under his arm and walked to the dining room for breakfast.

Satchen rose and bowed his head. "Good morning, Sir Alex," said Satchen.

"Good morning to you, sir," replied Alex.

"Alex, with all due respect, you may be a knight, but this is not a battlefield; it is my home. You will not sit at my table with weapons of war," stated Satchen.

"Understood, sir. I am truly sorry," Alex said as he unhooked his sword and dagger belt, placed it in the living room, and then returned to breakfast.

"Much better. Now, sit down, and eat," said Satchen.

"Yes, sir." Alex smiled with respect.

After they ate, Satchen and Alex joined the rest of the farewell group at the docks on the Bay of Anton. Yota, Gordon, and six other soldiers carried Brock's golden casket to a small floating barge. On the barge was a single seat upon which sat Jessica in a black veil. The royal condole, with King Anton and Princess Dora and two soldiers, drifted in front of the barge. A long, sleek vessel pulled up to the docks; Brock's parents and other family members boarded this craft, which pulled away from the dock and floated in the bay. Then a second, a third, and a fourth vessel of the same style as the first filled to capacity, pulled into the bay, and floated. Yota, Alex, Leappy, and Gordon boarded Leappy's condole and pulled away from the docks into the bay. Trumpets sounded, and Yota ordered his vessel to pull out to the city of Urbane.

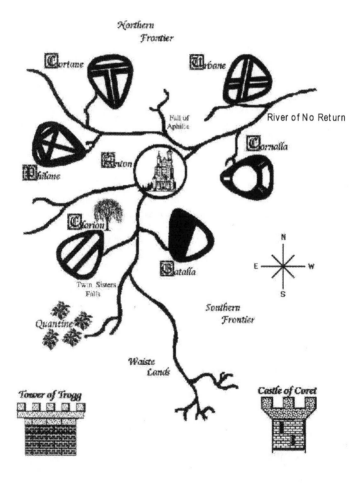

Slow as to not get too far ahead, the four long, sleek vessels pulled up behind in single file. Then Brock's barge was followed by the rest. The procession was slow moving. Not a single word was said the entire journey. After hours of silence, the small fleet could see the Tower of Urbane appear. The closer they came to Urbane, the larger the tower got. The Bay of Urbane was emptied. Along the shoreline, the citizens of Urbane stood as the fleet passed through. The only sound was Jessica's faint sobbing now and then.

An hour or so past the city of Urbane, the river began to narrow. Yota ordered his vessel to shore. Each vessel pulled in; every vessel went to the opposite shore of the river except Brock's barge. Two anchors were thrown overboard to hold the barge in place. The royal condole pulled up next to the barge for Jessica to board. She fell into Dora's arms in tears. The river's current had become stronger the closer they came to Urbane. The royal condole moored next to Leappy's.

"Alex, you and Gordon board the king's condole. Meet with Leappy and me at Brock's barge," ordered Yota.

Princess Dora began to sing in the elfin tongue. Her song was heavy and sad, and one by one, heads began to bow. The two condoles pulled up to the barge, Yota to the front and Alex at the rear. Yota drew his long blade and held it high in the air. Dora's song stopped, and every eye was on the barge. Yota, in a clear, commanding tone, spoke in his native language. At the end of each sentence came "Hail Brock!" He spoke for only a few moments. Swiftly in one motion, he cut the rope to the front anchor. Gordon pulled away from the barge. Since they had no rehearsal and Alex received no advice, he did as he felt. Why he felt the things he did was a mystery to him. He took off his helmet, stepped off his craft, walked up, and placed the helmet on Brock's chest plate on the lid o his coffin.

Alex placed his hand on the hilt of his sword and pounded his other hand on his chest in a fist. *A final salute to a true hero,* thought Alex. He stepped aboard Leappy's vessel and drew his sword from its sheath. He looked at

Yota, who in turn looked at King Anton, who looked deep into Jessica's eyes.

"May we let him return to Aurelie now, Jessica?" asked Anton. She drew a deep breath and then nodded yes. The king nodded to Yota, who nodded to Alex, who then with one clean motion severed the last anchor's rope. Brock's barge then floated freely to follow the current. The river drew the barge downstream. Every eye watched the barge become smaller and smaller until it drifted out of sight.

Slowly, the escort vessels were boarded and pulled out into the river at random. The royal condole and Leappy's craft made their way back upriver side by side. Once they neared Anton, Alex began to hear music and laughter. *Strange thing,* he thought, *after such a solemn event.*

Leappy placed a hand on Alex's shoulder. "It's a wake," said Leappy. "Brock would want us to be happy for him. The River of No Return has many tales, but they all end about the same," stated Leappy. "It is said Aurelie waits for all of us to return to her at river's end. Many have tried to find out. None has ever returned. That's how the river got its name. It is cause for laughter and celebration. Come on now, Alex," said Leappy.

"I'm sorry, Leappy. I feel very sad at the loss of a friend," responded Alex.

"As do we all. That is why we must abide in the belief our friend would have us be joyful and happy. Brock is or is soon to be with Queen Aurelie. His troubles are over, Alex. It is time to rejoice," finished Leappy.

"I'll try. Seems like an odd custom indeed," said Alex.

A large platform was set up in the park. Upon it was the king's throne and Princess Dora joined by Jessica. Prince Leroy's throne sat at the right hand of Anton, vacant. The prince was still on the battlefields.

Yota approached the king. He stopped at the edge of the platform until Anton waved for him to come forward. "My king, it is with respect for Brock and those closest to him I've come to Anton. I now ask pardon. I must return to my duties. I'll leave Gordon and Leappy for a short while, for Alex's sake. They, too, must join me in a few days' time. I've come to depend on them as soldiers as well as friends," said Yota.

"It will be as you say, Yota. It troubles me to see you go, but I know you must. May the love of Aurelie be with you, Yota. May an end come soon to this awful war. You are pardoned," finished Anton.

Yota waved Leappy, Gordon, and Alex over to him. They all came at a run. "My dearest friends, I now take leave to join my troops. Leappy, you and Gordon stay and visit with your pixies and Alex. Enjoy yourselves, please, for two days more. Then four days from now, I will expect you at my side on the Southern Frontier. Alex— Sir Alex—it has been both a heartwarming pleasure and an honor to see you again. It is with hope another time will come when we shall parley as before on the Island of Royal Children or under the Falls of Aphilia. If it is so, I will see you then. If not another day. I'm proud to have known you," said Yota.

Alex was touched, but he sensed worry and doubt in Yota. This was not at all like the warrior he knew. "May the love of your queen be with you, mighty warrior. That is my hope for you. We shall meet again, Yota. When may be a question, but there is no doubt about it," said Alex. Alex wasn't sure how it could be so steadfastly guaranteed, but it felt like the right thing to say.

"As you say," finished Yota.

Alex, Leappy, Gordon, Dona, Jessica and Princess Dora all begged the king for his pardon. They walked to the docks to see Yota off. Yota was already launched, and his torch was all that they could see as he made his way toward Gatalla.

Alex and the band of Royal Children watched until the torch was out of sight. They then split up into pairs: Gordon and Dona, Jessica with Leappy, and, of course, Alex and Dora. They strolled back to the edge of the park. Jessica and Leappy went back to the wake while the other four walked to the fountain, where they split up.

"Dora, would you mind a short walk to the riverfront?" asked Alex.

"That would be fine," answered Dora.

They walked out of sight of Gordon and Dona, who sat on a bench by the fountain. Dora took Alex by the hand. Alex began to blush a little, but he was getting used to the attention.

"Well, Alex, as before, you've seen a lot in a short time. What do you think?" asked Dora.

"The customs and traditions are different; that's true. All in all, though, I see their purpose and believe them to be of sound practice," said Alex.

"Come now, Alex, why get so philosophical?" asked Dora.

"I am very fond of your people, and they have good hearts and deep roots. I like that; that's all," ended Alex.

"Much better answer. We like you too." Dora smiled. "You have a few days before you must leave. Would you like to see or do anything special in that time?" asked Dora.

"Yes, in fact, I would. I would like another bonfire before Gordon and Leappy have to return to the front lines," said Alex.

"That is exactly what I wanted to hear. That can be arranged. Anything else?" Dora giggled.

"You … I mean, spend some time with you." Alex blushed.

"You are getting smarter," said Dora. Then they kissed and talked and kissed and talked some more.

"Alex! Alex, where are you?" yelled Leappy.

"I'm over here," said Alex.

"Come along. It's getting late. I'll meet you at me uncle's after you take the princess to the tower," stated Leappy.

"Yes, okay, I'll see you there shortly," replied Alex. "Are you ready, my lady?" he asked.

"Yes, my lord," Dora jested. They then rose and walked back to the Tower of Anton.

CHAPTER 16
UNTIL WE MEET AGAIN

"Leappy, what is going on on the Southern Frontier?" Asked Alex

"We fight, they fall back, we fortify the gain we make, then we fight again. It has been slow, but we are pushing Trogg and Coret back to the swamps. Little by little," said Leappy. "There have been reports that the Lord of Clarion, Sir Aldain, Gordon's father, has been taken to the dungeons of Coret's castle. Perhaps it is in hopes of ransom. As I say, they are reports; there has been no official word. It is difficult to keep Gordon in line. He wants to march straight in. Even if the reports of his father are true, to go too deep into that territory would be a fatal mistake. Trogg and Coret would circle in behind him, and he would be trapped along with those with him.

Once in the swamps, Coret and Trogg will take prisoners for hard labor. If the backbreaking work doesn't kill them, the filth and disease will.

"It is Yota's wish to push the brothers far enough back that they each retreat to their individual strongholds, then attack them one at a time. A second strategy is that once the brothers have retreated and given up fighting, we let them return to their cold, dark cities to lick their wounds. The second is more favored, for no one wants to enter the stench of their lands at all. The first, however, is the only sure way of knowing they won't try again in the future. If Sir Aldain is alive, we, of course, want to rescue him. Yota, with all respect, seems unsettled." Remarked Alex.

"Leappy, Yota expressed concern that Trogg was making things a little too easy. He feels the evil brothers have something going on that he is not aware of," said Alex.

"Yota, above all else, is a soldier. He knows by instinct when something is wrong. As to what he will do, I do not know. Come now; it's time to rest. Tomorrow, we'll all parley at the island before we must again part company," ended Leappy.

The night passed by, and Alex was awakened by Leappy. "Time to get the day started, Alex."

"Yes, okay, Leappy," Alex said.

After a quick breakfast, Leappy rushed Alex to his condole. "What's the big hurry?" asked Alex.

"We must gather the wood for tonight, set up the campsite, go back to Uncle Satchen's, clean up, and return in time for the others," Leappy said.

"I see," answered Alex.

"Besides, Gordon and I must start our journey back to the Southern Frontier tomorrow. Since it will be an early evening, I felt the sooner we could start, the longer we would have," Leappy responded.

"Makes sense," said Alex.

The two friends made their way to the island. Leappy took off in one direction, and Alex took off in another. Alex was picking up firewood as he felt sadness come over him. He knew when Leappy left, he would leave soon afterward. He felt troubled for his friends but knew it had to be this way.

Between Alex and Leappy, they stacked more than enough firewood for two bonfires. Then they finished up and headed back to Uncle Satchen's. The pixies had spent the morning preparing a meal; they knew no one was going to eat.

The band of Royal Children met on the docks a little

before midday. Gordon helped Leappy with a barrel of ale as Alex helped the princess aboard her craft. Gordon, Leappy, and Dona boarded Leappy's vessel. Jessica joined Dora; as they pulled away from the docks, hardly a word was spoken.

Once they landed on the island, the pixies spread out a quilt. They placed the picnic meal on it while Gordon and Leappy carried the barrel of ale. Alex started a small fire. As the group settled in, the silence continued. Leappy, Gordon, and Alex began talking about the war and the Battle of Clarion, filling Alex in on what happened after the giant spider picked him up.

Dora, Dona, and Jessica tried to console one another on being left alone. Soon, Jessica spoke up. "You mighty warriors, get over here. Is it not enough to have lived through such things that you must talk about them over and over again?"

With no words in defense, Gordon said, "Sorry."

"I should think so," Dona said.

Alex sat down next to Dora on the quilt, and the others joined. As they tried to eat and drink, it seemed nearly impossible to be merry. Soon, Alex stood, held up his schooner, and said, "To Leappy and Gordon—may the queen's love see them home quickly and unharmed."

"Hear, hear!" yelled the band of Royal Children.

Then Leappy stood. "To Alex, my friend—may you live to be very old. With the love of our queen, we wish you safe passage home. Also, if at all possible, we wish a future visit under much more pleasant circumstances."

Again there came a round of "Hear, hear!"

It remained silent awhile before Princess Dora spoke up. "If you please, my friends, I think it has been a very full past few days. Perhaps we all need time to ourselves before we can band together as a group. I know I am pretty drained from all the activity and would like to return home," Dora stated.

Leappy spoke next. "Jessica, Dona, Gordon, and I will clean up here, if you would see Princess Dora home, Alex."

"Of course," Alex answered.

Dora looked out across the water to the Bay of Anton. Her first words since leaving the island were "Thank you, Alex."

Alex helped her step down from the vessel onto the docks. "You are very quiet," said Alex.

"Yes, Alex, I'm sorry. I'm also sad to see your visit come to an end." Dora sighed.

"I still have a few days, Dora. I knew when I came

there would be a time to leave again. It's not easy for me either," Alex replied.

"Yes, Alex, I know. I just have these feelings running so deep inside me; it's hard to explain," Dora said.

"Then don't. I mean, you don't have to explain. I believe I can understand," Alex said.

"Can you, Alex? Can you really understand? I am a princess, a daughter to a king—a very old king whose people are at war. If anything should happen to my father, how could I handle such a responsibility? You'll be gone, and who am I to turn to, Alex? Who then?" Dora repeated.

"Please, Princess, I must believe everything in the kingdom is going to turn out just fine. Yota and his generals will stamp out the threat of Trogg and Coret. Your father will be refreshed when the worry of war has passed and live many more years to come. Prince Leroy will also return," Alex stated.

"Then what, Alex? What am I to do? My heart is wherever you are. It's by your side I choose to be. Is it not possible?" Dora asked.

"I don't have all the answers. You must believe I'd stay with you forever if I could. At this time, I don't see how that can be, perhaps never. I don't have the power to change that. Nor do you."

Dora began to cry. It touched Alex so deeply he had tears in his eyes. He held the princess, trying to be of some comfort to her.

Suddenly, Dora pushed Alex away. "You can watch from here, Alex. I'll walk the rest of the way alone. I must get used to being alone. I may or may not see you before you leave."

Alex wanted to speak but held his tongue. The princess turned and walked toward the Tower of Anton. *Saint Peter,* thought Alex, *what did I do?*

Alex waited for Leappy and the others on the docks. When they returned, the band of Royal Children split up. Leappy and Alex began their short walk to Satchen's. Leappy was as helpful as he could be by listening to Alex talk about Dora. "Alex, my friend, in times like these, things are thought impossible. They are just that: impossible. Nothing and no one can change things from being what they are. Tomorrow will come. Wherever it may find us, it will surely come. It's obvious your feelings for our princess run deep. Remember, from time to time, you must come up for air."

"What?" Alex questioned.

"I'm saying you must do what life demands of you first. Then if time allows, you may do some of what you want. Spending too much time in deep water, thinking and worrying about things you have no control over, will waste your time for living. You must break away from feeling frustrated. Take time to breathe; live your life as it happens. Don't live how someone else would have you live or even place too much effort on what you would rather do. Be happy, Alex. For now, you belong above ground. For now, you can't change that. Once there, perhaps you'll discover more of your place in your lifetime. Perhaps one day you'll return and claim your heart's desire. Perhaps, Alex; just perhaps," Leappy ended.

"Thank you, Leappy. I will truly miss your friendship and council."

Alex never slept more than a few minutes at a time that night. The dawn came, and Alex was slow in getting up and dressed. Satchen and Leappy were finishing up breakfast by the time Alex joined them.

Leappy looked into Alex's eyes and said, "Good morning."

Alex halfheartedly replied, "Good morning to you both."

"Well, Alex, what do you have planned for your last few days here?" Leappy asked.

"Don't have any plans, really. In fact, I may leave a day early," Alex said.

"That's tomorrow in your time, Alex. You'll be back a day earlier than your grandfather," Leappy commented.

"Yes, I know. I'm not really sure of what to do," Alex said.

"I'll wait for you in the park," Leappy stated.

"I'll be along shortly," Alex said. Satchen asked Alex what was bothering him. "I have to go," Alex said.

"Yes, go on," Satchen replied.

"That's it, sir. I have to go, and I don't want to," Alex finished.

"Of course, Alex. Now that quantine grows wild again, don't you think you'll return someday?" Satchen asked.

"It's not that, sir. I mean, yes, of course, I'd like to return. *Return to what?* I wonder," Alex said.

"Alex, none of us above- or belowground knows what tomorrow may bring. You must live for today. All any living thing has is the present. You are troubled beyond your ability to control. What becomes of this kingdom, your home, yourself, or me is not for you to decide. You can only accept what comes," Satchen said.

"That's hard for me, sir."

"It's hard sometimes for us all. Come now, Alex; put on a smile, and enjoy what little time you have left with Leappy. I'll see you before they leave for Gatalla," Satchen finished.

CHAPTER 17
FARE THEE WELL

Leappy was standing by the fountain in the middle of the park when Alex arrived. "Alex, listen."

Alex listened. "I don't hear anything but the sound of the fountain," Alex said.

"Yes, Princess Dora is not singing in the tower. Never before has she missed a single morning," Leappy announced.

Alex looked up at the top of the tower. The balcony was empty. "Should we check on her?" Alex asked.

"No, that is not in order. Perhaps we will see her at my farewell," Leappy stated. "Come on; let's find Gordon."

The pair headed down a path that was unfamiliar to Alex. Small cottages lined both sides of the path. Alex heard his and Leappy's names being called. Then he spotted Gordon and Dona. They were sitting on a swing on the front porch of a brightly painted cottage. Gordon and Dona then stood at the gate when Alex and Leappy walked up to them. Dona hugged Gordon and said she would see him at his farewell. Alex wanted to ask her about Dora, but he watched his manners.

"Come, my friends; let's spend our last few hours together," Gordon said. The three sat back on the porch and talked of past events and when they would see each other again.

The day seemed to pass slowly for Alex. His mind was not always on the conversation at hand. In fact, he stared into the middle of nowhere, and he didn't hear Gordon bid him off.

Leappy stood in front of Alex and clapped his hands. Alex looked up at Leappy, who said, "Gordon said good-bye."

"Oh, yes, see you soon, Gordon."

Leappy and Alex returned to Uncle Satchen's, where Leappy changed into his soldier attire. "Well, that's about it," Leappy said.

"That's about what?" Alex asked.

"Oh, my little vacation. I want you never to forget, Alex, you are my friend and I am yours. If I had a brother, I would want him to be like you," Leappy said.

Alex took it as a large compliment. "Leappy, I feel as though I should be leaving with you and Gordon," Alex stated.

That afternoon, another feast and ball was conducted in the park. The food was plentiful, and laughter filled the air. Alex searched for the princess. He didn't find her anywhere. Leappy and Gordon were kept busy by friends and family.

Finally, Alex left the festivities to walk along the river's shore. He felt troubled, not sure of anything at all. He wanted to be home, but at the same time, he wanted to be beside his friends. He felt terribly alone. Not even his dearest friend, Dora, was there to talk matters over with.

The light was turning a pale blue when Roe found Alex. "Alex, Leappy and Gordon have sent me for you."

"Yes, I'm coming," Alex replied.

Gordon and Leappy were aboard a flat-bottomed boat when Alex arrived. Alex boarded the small craft.

"Well, Alex, this is until we meet again, which I hope is very soon," Leappy said.

Gordon stood and saluted Alex, who returned the gesture. "There is no one around, Gordon."

"I know. It is still deserving, though, old friend," Gordon finished.

Alex hugged Gordon and then Leappy, and biting his lower lip, he stepped off the vessel. "Be off with you. May the love of Aurelie bring you both back home safe again." Alex watched them push off and head downriver. He stood silent on the dock until their torch was out of sight.

"Alex, is there anything I can do?" Roe asked. "They will return."

"Yes, Roe, I must trust that they will. Can you tell me anything about the princess?"

"Yes, but I am sworn to secrecy, Alex."

"It's okay, Roe. I won't ask you to break your word."

"Alex, I can venture this much: you may not see the princess again before you leave."

"Why?" Alex asked.

"That I cannot say," Roe answered.

"You don't know why?" Alex quizzed.

"Yes, I do, but I cannot say," Roe replied.

"Well, if that is the way of it, I wish for you to take me home. Tomorrow isn't soon enough, but it will have to do," Alex said.

"Very well, Alex. I'll meet with you at Satchen's at first light. If I might make one suggestion, Alex—" Roe said.

"Yes, what is it?" Alex snapped.

"See the king. It would not be polite to leave without a word," Roe replied.

"True, I shall do that, and thank you, Roe, for everything."

Alex hung his head and slowly made his way to the king's chambers. The guards snapped to attention. Alex reluctantly returned their salutes. He asked one of them to announce he would like an audience with Anton.

"At this hour, sir?" questioned a guard.

"Yes, now!" Alex said.

"As you say, Sir Alex."

The king was preparing to retire but granted an audience for Alex. When Alex entered the throne room, upon his throne was Anton. "Come in, Alex," Anton said.

Alex bowed and approached the throne. "King Anton, it is with a heavy heart that I come to bid you farewell," Alex stated.

"Farewell so soon, Alex? Don't you have time left you could spend in Anton?" the king asked.

"Yes, but my friends have left, and I cannot see the princess. You, Great King, shall be the last next to Satchen and Roe. It has been a most eventful visit. There has been so much sorrow and so much laughter. I shall cherish these memories always," Alex said.

"Remember us, Alex, for we shall never forget the human lad who became a knight to the king. It is my honor to have known you. Let it be known you are welcome here always," Anton replied.

"Thank you, Great King. I'm not sure everyone here in your kingdom feels that way. Just the same, there is a special place for your world in my heart. I shall always feel like a part of Anton. Perhaps at a better time I shall return. Please forgive me if I am out of line, sir. Could you tell your daughter I shall miss her most of all? If it were up to me, I'd stay forever. It's not yet clear to me how that could be."

"I see. I guessed this much," Anton said. "That is, that you and Dora have grown fond of each other. In my years, Alex, I have seen many strange things, unbelievable things to some. It is the heart of anyone that makes them who they are. You, Alex, are a great hero to my people. I should be happy to call you one of my own. I don't believe there is any law written anywhere that you must be a leprechaun to love a leprechaun. Are you following me, Alex?" the king asked.

"I think so, sir."

"Go home, Alex, and grow. Return as often as you like. To me, you are Sir Alex, my knight, who has sworn to defend my people and our way of life. I am proud to know you. We will wait for your return. May the love of our queen go with you."

Alex stood tall and saluted King Anton. They stared into each other's eyes. It was as if they knew it was the last time they would speak. Alex turned from the king.

Once back at Satchen's, Alex put his armor and new clothes in the closet. When he closed the closet door, Alex mumbled to himself, "A knight to King Anton. Me—how could I ever think that this was meant for me?"

Alex spent breakfast with Satchen. They tried to comfort each other, which had little effect on how Alex felt. They parted at Satchen's door. Alex watched the door close. When he turned around, there stood Roe.

"Are you ready, Alex?" Roe asked.

"No, I'm not ready, but still, I must go," Alex snapped.

They made their way to the docks and boarded Roe's flat-bottomed vessel. As they pushed off the dock, Alex froze. Dora atop the Tower of Anton began her song to the children of Aurelie. Alex looked to the tower to see his princess waving good-bye to him as she sang. Alex stood and waved back as he left Anton Bay. The tower shrank out of sight, but never out of mind or heart.

THE END

Printed in the United States
By Bookmasters